PUFFIN BOOKS

SPY DOG
GUNPOWDER PLOT

Man's best friend? *Deffo*. Ever since we adopted her from the RSPCA, Lara and I have been besties. We've got loads in common. We both drool when it's nearly tea time, we both think sausages are yummy, we love snoozing in front of the telly and we both hate vacuum cleaners.

We've shared so many adventures and here we are, at the final one, an epic finale where we find out whether everyone lives happily ever after. Or not. I couldn't decide so I wrote three endings and read them to my dog. She didn't like the zombie one (too much blood) or the 'falling into a raging river and down a waterfall' one (too soggy), so we plumped for something more, erm, *unusual*?

Fingers and paws crossed that you love our final adventure. Thank you for sharing our journey.

Andy and Lara

andy@artofbrilli

Books by Andrew Cope

Spy Dog series in reading order
Spy Dog
Captured!
Unleashed!
Superbrain
Rocket Rider
Secret Santa
Teacher's Pet
Rollercoaster!
Brainwashed
Mummy Madness
Storm Maker
Gunpowder Plot

Spy Pups series in reading order
Treasure Quest
Prison Break
Circus Act
Danger Island
Survival Camp

Spy Cat series in reading order
Summer Shocker!
Blackout!
Safari

Spy Dog Joke Book

SPY DOG
GUNPOWDER PLOT

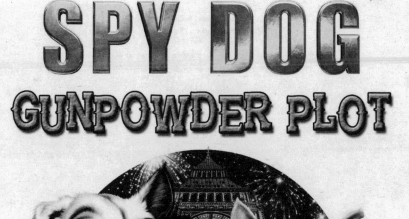

ANDREW COPE

Illustrated by James de la Rue

PUFFIN

PUFFIN BOOKS

UK | USA | Canada | Ireland | Australia
India | New Zealand | South Africa

Puffin Books is part of the Penguin Random House group of companies
whose addresses can be found at global.penguinrandomhouse.com.

www.penguin.co.uk
www.puffin.co.uk
www.ladybird.co.uk

First published 2016
001

Text copyright © Andrew Cope, 2016
Illustrations copyright © James de la Rue, 2016

The moral right of the author and illustrator has been asserted

Set in 15/18 pt Bembo Book MT Std
Typeset by Jouve (UK), Milton Keynes
Printed in Great Britain by Clays Ltd, St Ives plc

A CIP catalogue record for this book is available from the British Library

ISBN: 978–0–141–36999–0

All correspondence to:
Puffin Books
Penguin Random House Children's
80 Strand, London WC2R 0RL

www.greenpenguin.co.uk

For my favourite family. Thank you.

Contents

Introduction: The Next Generation

Four puppies sat with their chests out and eyes agog as their mum put the finishing touches to their dinner. The wafting smell of tuna pasta bake had attracted their attention and they were swarming round her feet, except Tyrone who was sitting in the corner where he knew the dog bowl would soon be arriving. Delilah licked the drool from her lips. 'Is it ready yet, Mum?' she yowled. 'I'm starving!'

'Me too,' yelped Geronimo. 'And it smells so yummy. Look at my tail. It's got a life of its own.'

'Patience, pups,' woofed Star, biting on a spatula and scooping dollops of pasta bake into a bowl. 'It's got to cool.'

The puppies had been attending the professor's special school for pets, but they hadn't learned patience. Their tails swished and tongues lolled as their mum waited for the steam to stop rising.

'It's coming, it's coming,' panted Bella as Star balanced the bowl on her paws and started towards the corner of the room. 'Out of the way, kids,' she warned. 'We don't want food spilled everywhere.' The pups didn't care about spillage. Four hungry puppies cleared a small space and then sat, just like they'd been taught. Star bent down and placed the bowl on the floor. Four pairs of eyes ogled the food and then their mum, waiting for the instruction. Delilah had a huge droplet of drool dangling from her lips.

'For what we are about to eat . . .' began Star.

'We are truly thankful,' woofed the puppies as quickly as they could before they attacked the bowl, heads down and tails up, their bodies wriggling in excitement. Dinner-time was a messy affair. Tyrone was the smallest, which is why he always thought ahead and bagsied a front row place. Star smiled as she watched him hold his position in the crowd, chomping his fair share of the best bits of tuna.

'Manners, everyone,' woofed Star, her words falling on deaf ears.

Uncle Spud looked up from his newspaper, smiling at his nephews and nieces and wiping away a bit of his own drool. He knew that he and his sister would be eating a bit later but he couldn't help hoping the pups might leave a morsel. He looked at the wriggling bodies fighting for space.

Fat chance, he thought.

Star and Spud loved living with the Cook family but, if the truth be known, it hadn't been the same since Ben had left for university.

'It's such a shame that the kids had to grow up,' sighed Star. 'It seems only yesterday that Ben, Sophie and Ollie were young and playful and we had all those adventures.'

Spud wagged hard as his brain ran some images from the good old days when he and Star were puppies and their mum was the world's first ever Spy Dog. He looked at the ginger cat, curled on the chair. His ripped left ear and bent tail were clues to more exciting times. Spud couldn't help but wince because every time Shakespeare yawned, which was a lot, his jaw clicked and he yowled in pain.

That broken jaw never did mend properly, thought Spud.

'But it was worth it, sis. We were the best secret-agent team evs.'

His sister sighed. 'They were good times,' she agreed. 'But today's not bad either. Sure Ben has gone but Sophie's in Year Ten and Ollie's doing OK in Year Seven. The kids have grown up and so have we! Look at us: from adventurous pups to fully grown dogs. We

couldn't have found a better family or a better life. I mean, how many dogs get to be part of an elite team of undercover agents? How many dogs have captured evil baddies and saved the world?'

The only sound was the metal bowl scraping across the tiles as the pups' enthusiastic eating chased it across the room. Spud and Star were lost in the same thought.

'Mum sure was awesome,' said Star.

'You mean GM451,' chuckled Star. 'That's what the mad prof used to call her. Or LARA – Licensed Assault and Rescue Animal. I reckon she's captured more baddies than you've had hot dinners.' She glanced at her brother who immediately sucked in his furry belly. 'Well, perhaps not,' she corrected. 'But she was the most amazing mutt the world has ever known. Number One canine.'

'Do you ever wish we could go back to those times?' asked Spud.

Star smiled a huge doggy grin. 'They were great days, bro, but I have other things on my plate right now. Like washing up and then homework!' she said, eyeing the four sticking-up backsides.

'How about you do the washing up and I'll sort the homework,' he suggested, and ten minutes later, while his sister was up to her elbows in bubbles, Uncle Spud was in charge of his beloved nieces and nephews. Spud's plan was to get the pups' homework started and then sneak off for his own tea. He had his eye on a jacket tatty with cheese and beans.

Oh, and that piece of cheesecake I've seen in the fridge, wrapped in clingfilm. Looks like it needs eating, he thought to himself.

The girls had been easy to sort. They were working on a team history project about spies through the ages, so Bella was Googling while

Delilah took notes. Uncle Spud knew that would keep them quiet at least until they started arguing over who would be in charge of putting the PowerPoint presentation together.

Geronimo was less academic.

More of an all-action dog, thought Spud.

So although he was part of the spies through the ages team, Spud had asked him to go and get dressed up as a spy and snoop round the neighbourhood.

'Listen in,' he said, 'in secret. Come back in half an hour and report your findings to your team.' He chuckled to himself as he watched Geronimo tiptoeing out of the back door, magnifying glass in his paws.

'Which just leaves you, little fella,' said Spud, looking down at Ty. The black puppy looked up at his uncle and wrinkled his nose. 'I can't be bothered, Uncle Spud. School is boring. I'd rather be outside. You know, playing.'

'What, like chasing a stick?' asked Spud.

'Or a ball,' wagged his nephew. 'Or even a cat, maybe . . .' His tail picked up some speed and his eyes shone.

Spud nodded. 'I know what you mean, Ty. I really do. Chasing a ball is great fun.' He eyed the sleeping cat. 'And mogs, even more fun. Although, personally, I wouldn't pick a fight with that one. He's a black belt in karate.'

'Really?' asked Ty. 'Shakespeare doesn't look very tough.'

The ginger cat opened one eye. 'I'm listening, young pup,' he purred. 'First rule of spy club: ears open, even when your eyes are closed.'

'They say cats have nine lives,' said Spud. 'Well, we've calculated that Shakespeare has had fourteen.'

'Fifteen,' corrected the puss, opening the other eye and yawning. 'Ouch!' he howled as his jaw clicked. 'I must make an appointment to get that seen to.' The ginger cat stretched and changed position, with his white feet tucked under, as if he were floating on the sofa. 'But school matters, little dude,' he said, sleepily. 'Most pets don't go to school. So the fact that you do makes you special.' He did a long blink, as though the effort of keeping his eyes open was beyond him. 'And yours is not any old school. Oh my goodness, no.' There was another long blink and then the lids closed. 'You go to Spy School.'

'That puss is right.' Spud nodded. 'Professor Cortex is the best of the best. You can already play the piano, little fella. I mean, the internet's alive with silly dogs and cats, doing funny stuff. But you're the only puppy on the planet with grade three piano.'

'And I'm a free reader.'

'And a very good writer,' added his uncle. 'So let's check your writing homework.'

Spud waited patiently as Ty nosed his laptop open and took a pencil in his mouth. He tapped a few keys and his emails opened up.

'Thith one,' he said out of the side of his mouth. 'I've goth to writh a thtory.'

Spud reached for his spectacles and peered at it. 'Write about a superhero who has an adventure that makes your spine tingle with excitement,' he read, 'and that ends on a cliffhanger.'

'I'm thtuck,' woofed Ty, through a mouthful of pencil. 'I wath going to do Thpiderman and then I thought about the Hulk. I mean, he wath angry and green and all that. But those thtories have already been done in comicth and filmth.'

Spud nodded, an idea whirring in his head. 'What if you wrote about a *real* superhero, not a fictional one?'

9

Ty laughed, the pencil clattering on to the table. 'Superheroes aren't real, Uncle Spud. They're characters in comic books.'

'I knew a real one,' added the cat, both green eyes suddenly boring into Tyrone. 'Remember all those bedtime stories Uncle Spud told you. About the spy pets team? Our leader was a superhero, for sure.' Ty noticed the cat had gone from fast asleep to 'fast awake' in a tenth of a second. His feet weren't tucked in – he was standing, his one and a half ears pointing tall.

Spud was wagging. 'Puss is right. Why don't you write about your grandma? She was the most amazing superhero the world has ever known.'

Ty was nodding. 'I like the sound of that, Uncle Spud.' He rummaged for his pencil, holding it in his paws. 'But which story, Uncle Spud? You've told me so many! And I've read so many newspaper clippings. There was the rocket one. Or the submarine one where you nearly died! Or when you had to break into prison to help that evil baddie escape. That was amaaaazing! Or the one where you had to be in a circus?'

Spud looked at the cat. They both knew. 'Grandma Lara had many fabulous adventures, Ty. But her last one was a spine-tingling epic. Why don't you write about that one?'

'Thanks, Uncle Spud, that's a brilliant idea. My superhero wasn't green and angry. She was black, white and kind and her superpower was catching evil baddies. And guess what, Uncle Spud, you were there too, when you were a pup. Oh my gosh, this is soooo exciting.'

Shakespeare sank into a cushion and closed his eyes, his gappy front teeth showing in a smile of satisfaction. 'Good choice,' he purred.

Spud smiled a doggie grin as he watched Ty

open a Word document and grip the pencil tightly in his teeth. He glanced at his uncle, took a deep breath and started tapping at the keyboard.

'Based on a true story . . .'

1. Face to Face

It started in Hurtmore Mega-Max Ultimate Security Prison. The guard slid the bolt and opened the hatch. The prisoner saw eyes peering in and then a mouth. 'Big,' said the lips, 'you've been summoned by the medical team. Six-monthly check-up.'

The prisoner sat on his bed and waited, listening as keys were inserted, locks opened and bolts unbolted. Three burly guards stood at the door.

'We're waiting,' said the broadest of the men.

The prisoner smiled from behind his protective mask as he raised himself to his feet. *Five years in solitary confinement has been so boring*, he thought as he shuffled towards the door, his ankle chains clinking as he walked. *Locked up for twenty-three life sentences and this is going to be my last day.*

One guard led the way, the other two bringing up the rear. Even with ankle chains and handcuffs on, Big was still a threat. The criminal couldn't help a nod and a wave at the cameras that tracked their progress towards the

hospital wing. The men walked in silence before finally arriving at a door.

'Ah, my therapy appointment,' purred the master criminal from behind the orange mask. 'To check I'm still alive and dangerous.'

One of the guards knocked, opened the door and led Mr Big in. The door was bolted and the other two stood guard outside. They were taking no chances.

The room had a desk with two chairs. Mr Big was pushed into one of the chairs and a nervous-looking therapist sat opposite. The prison officer took his place in the doorway, guarding the only possible escape route. The doctor fiddled nervously with his pen and looked up from a wad of notes. 'How's things?' he asked.

'Apart from the mask, things are just hunky-dory,' growled the criminal.

'The mask is for protection,' said the doctor, staring into a pair of insane eyes, one blue and one glass. 'Protection for *us*, from *you*,' he reminded.

There was a pause. 'I've been having a lot of quality time to myself. It's given me plenty of time to think,' said Big, staring unblinkingly at the doctor. 'And reflect.'

'Thinking about turning over a new leaf?' asked the therapist. 'Or maybe reflecting on being a good boy from now on?'

The prisoner's eyes smiled. 'Not exactly, doc. I've been having some thoughts about pulling off one more crime. Something so big that it'd make the world sit up and take notice. And so evil that it'd make me famous.'

The doctor scribbled his words down on a pad. 'One more crime, eh? And what kind of crime would that be?'

There was a hollow laugh from behind the mask. 'Top secret,' he growled. 'If I told yer, I'd have to kill yer. And that'd make a terrible mess in this office. So let's just say it will be my swansong. I'm planning on going out with a bang.'

The therapist smiled. 'Planning? What's the point in planning? Don't you see the problem, Big?'

'I don't like the word *problem*,' interrupted the criminal. 'It's so negative. I prefer *solution*. There's always a *solution* to everything.'

'Your *problem*,' emphasized the therapist, 'is that you're locked up in the world's highest security prison. For the rest of your life. So there's no swansong, Big. There's no last job and no going out with a bang. How could you commit a crime from in here?'

Mr Big nodded. 'By finding a solution,' he said.

The therapist clicked his pen nervously. Big

was under lock and key, with a protective face mask, ankle and handcuffs, there was a burly guard standing in the doorway and two more standing outside and yet he still had an uneasy feeling.

'You have to be realistic,' said the doctor, trying to sound brave. Some situations are impossible.'

'Wrong again, amigo,' growled the voice from behind the mask. 'I find that impossible just takes a little longer. Isn't that right, Gus?'

Mr Big heard a thud as the dart hit the therapist and he slumped in his chair. 'Quickly, Gus,' hissed Mr Big, 'as per the plan. And get this bloomin' mask off of me.' The fake security guard unlocked the mask to reveal a huge grin on the criminal's sweaty face. The men worked quickly to release the cuffs and Mr Big swapped clothes with the therapist and took his ID badge. Mr Big then chained the wrists and ankles of the sleeping man and fixed the orange mask in place. 'That's his mug sorted; now what about mine?' purred the criminal. 'You did the 3D printing, as requested?'

The security guard rolled up his trouser leg and retrieved a clear plastic bag. 'It's a bit fiddly, boss,' he said, 'but, as you can see from mine, they're very lifelike.'

Mr Big smiled at the handsome guard, knowing that he was wearing a 3D printed mask and that underneath were the gnarled face and cauliflower ears of one of the ugliest men he'd ever worked with.

'Yours,' said Gus, handing Mr Big what looked like a plastic mould. 'The trick is to smooth it so there aren't any wrinkles.' Mr Big waited while Gus smoothed the plastic over his face and patted it into place. Mr Big stepped in front of the mirror and let out a low whistle. He looked exactly like the therapist.

Mr Big gave the thumbs up. 'Now for a little noise and then we will be on our way, Gussy-my-boy.'

'Oi, you!' yelled Gus, 'I told you to sit down.' He banged his fist hard on the desk and, right on cue, the guards burst in. They saw the therapist looking a little frightened and the masked criminal slumped in a chair. The security guard was rubbing his hand. 'I had to hit him,' explained Gus. 'He was threatening the doc. He's unconscious. I guess that means I'll have to write it up in a report. Can you guys carry him back to his cell while I escort the doc off the premises?'

The real guards dragged the unconscious medic back to Mr Big's cell and laid him on the bed. As the keys turned, locks were shut and bolts bolted, Mr Big flashed the therapist's ID card at the lady in the gatehouse. The pretend security guard and fake medic stood in the car park and Mr Big inhaled the fresh air.

'Freedom's never smelled so good,' he said to Gus. He checked his jacket pocket and found the doctor's car keys. He clicked the fob and some lights flashed. 'My transport, I presume,' he said to Gus. 'I'll see you back at base.'

The world's most wanted criminal saluted the security team as he pulled out of the prison car park. 'The problem with the modern world,' he said to himself, 'is too much negative thinking. There's always a solution.'

This particular 'impossible' had taken him five years. His next 'impossible' was going to be the biggest crime the world had ever seen. 'But first,' he growled, 'there's the little matter of a dog.'

2. Secret Stuff

Spy Dog looked across at her pups and wagged. She noticed that even Spy Cat's tail was swishing with excitement. *Such is the power of the professor's enthusiasm*, she thought.

The old fellow was hopping from foot to foot in what the animals called the Mad Professor Dance. Lara had been through the professor's top secret Spy School programme so she knew all the signs. *The faster he hops, the greater the excitement*, she smiled, *and that's a very fast hop!*

Lara noticed the children were grinning too. 'Hey, Prof, quit dancing and tell us what you've come up with.'

'Well, young Sophie,' he began, eyes gleaming and fingers fiddling, 'I think I've outdone myself. Something for everyone. Where to start?'

Ben was the oldest of the children and he often had the coolest head. 'Start by calming down,' he soothed.

'Yes, quite,' agreed the old man, fingers still flapping. 'Calming down.' He nodded furiously. 'Calming down is a good thing. And while I'm calming, give me your mobile, Master Benjamin.'

Ben rummaged in his pocket and handed it over. 'As I thought,' tutted the scientist, 'nothing but a normal mobile phone.' He went to the sink and filled a bowl with cold water. 'In perfect working order until this happens,' he said, plunging it into the bowl.

'Hey!' complained the boy. 'That's my phone. You've ruined it!'

'Oh completely,' agreed the professor, pulling the dripping phone from the water. 'Useless.'

Ben looked very cross, his scowl prompting the professor to rummage in his own pocket. 'Here,' he said, 'you need this *next generation* phone.' He handed Ben another mobile phone. 'It has an underwater app,' explained the professor. 'See this here?' he said, peering over his spectacles. 'Press it like so and the app is activated.' He took the phone from Ben and tossed it into the bowl with a splash.

'Hey – that's not fair,' said Ben. 'That's two phones ruined.'

'No, no,' said the professor, shaking his head and rolling his sleeve up to retrieve the phone from the bottom of the bowl. He shook the water off and tapped a number before putting it to his ear. 'Hello, Mrs Cook, yes it's me, Maximus. I'm just ringing to prove this phone works.'

There was a pause as he listened. 'Of course they're safe,' he said with a nervous chuckle.

I've got the three children, dogs and mog right here in front of me.'

There was another pause as he listened. 'She's worried about you,' he mouthed, pointing at the kids. 'Oh, I wouldn't dream of getting them into any mischief. In fact, Mrs C, I'm about to introduce them to an invention that might change your life.' He listened for a few seconds. The dogs' keen ears could pick up some shouting. 'Yes, yes, what's that . . . I think I'm losing you . . . helloooo . . . goodbye,' he said, ending the call.

'So the phone works when it's wet,' said Ben. 'That is pretty cool. I mean some phones just die if they get rained on.'

'It's a lot more than pretty cool, Master Benjamin,' corrected the professor. 'Not only does it mean that your phone will work if you drop it down the toilet . . .'

'Urgh,' said Ollie. 'It'd have poo on it. And you'd get it in your ear . . .'

'Quite,' frowned the professor. 'But it also opens up a whole new world of mobile communications.' He looked at the bemused faces. 'Don't you see?'

'See what?' asked Sophie.

'You can phone somebody from *underwater*!' gasped the professor, his glasses steaming up in excitement. 'No other phone can do that.' The professor waited, nodding his head, his eyes pleading for someone to punch the air at his genius. His nodding gradually ceased as all he saw were shaking heads and furrowed brows.

'Professor,' said Ollie, 'people can't actually talk underwater. What would I do, phone Mum from the deep end of the swimming pool and go, 'Bloob bloob blurrrrb bloob,' he said, waving his arms around to make pretend underwater bubbles.

The professor's brow remained furrowed. 'I see,' he said, scrabbling for his notebook. He licked the end of his pencil and scribbled 'cannot speak underwater'. 'That's an interesting thought.'

Sophie noticed the Mad Professor Dance had stopped. The little girl felt a bit sorry for him. His inventions were brilliant, but sometimes excitement got the better of him and he didn't think them through. 'Anything else, Prof?' she asked, trying to sound enthusiastic.

'But of course,' insisted the professor. 'In

fact, I think the dogs will be wagging when they see what I've got for them. Follow me.'

'Is it an automatic waffle maker or maybe a new cheesecake recipe, with real Cheddar and real cake?' yapped Spud in delight.

The professor couldn't understand dog language but he had become a good reader of body language. 'Your enthusiasm, agent canines, tells me that you want a gadget for pets. Let me guess, something you can use on missions? And, Agent Spud, your extreme wagging means you want some chips, or maybe a double cheese-burger? With bacon, perhaps?'

'Oh my gosh, he's invented a mind-reading gadget, sis,' wagged Spud.

'Follow me back to the lab and I'll introduce you to my finest . . . and smallest gadget.' The professor turned on his heel and clopped speedily along the white corridor and back to his inventing lab. He checked a couple of bubbling potions, tasting one of them, and scribbled a few notes on an iPad before turning his attention back to the children and animals. He tapped at his laptop. 'I'm going to beam a picture on to the wall,' he explained, 'and it might seem a little scary.'

The professor tapped a key and a terrifying image of an alien appeared on the wall. It was black with huge teeth and massive claws, like one Ben had seen in a film he knew he wasn't old enough to watch.

'Cooooool,' said Ollie. 'Are we being invaded by aliens? Are they going to chomp us with their massive teeth and is their blood made of acid?'

'It's not actually an alien,' soothed the professor. 'And, double good news, it's not massive. In fact, it's tiny. That image is magnified ten thousand times. The actual creature is almost invisible to the human eye.' The professor pulled a small glass box from his pocket.

'Let me introduce you to *Ctenocephalides canis bionicus*,' announced the professor, handing round the box and a magnifying glass.

'Obviously that name is a bit of a mouthful so I need to think of something easier. Is *Ctenocephalides canis electronicus* any better? You see the *Ctenocephalides canis* bit is Greek for dog flea but I just added the *bionicus* bit, to indicate that it's electronic rather than an actual *flea* flea, so to speak.' The scientist looked round the room at the bemused faces.

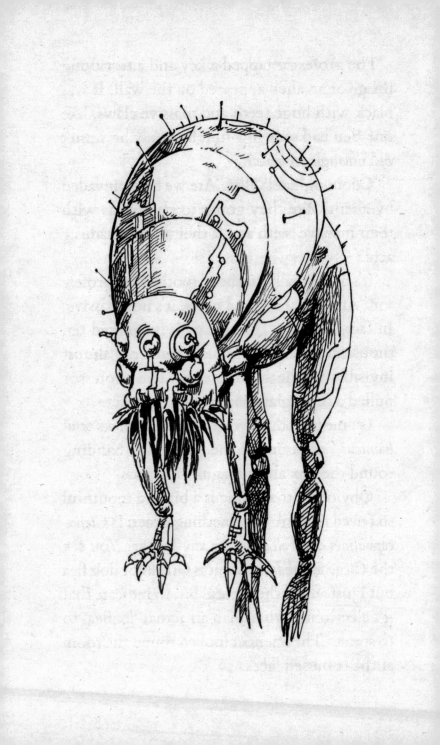

'I think we should call him Bob,' suggested Ollie.

'Quite,' said the professor, his wincing face disagreeing with his nodding head. '*Cteno-cephalides canis bionicus . . .*'

'Bob,' reminded Ollie.

'Erm . . . Bob,' said the professor, the word getting stuck in his mouth, 'is my latest and I have to say, very best invention.' The glass box was passed round and Ollie shook it violently, making the electronic flea rattle. 'Luckily it's quite sturdy,' said the professor, snatching the box from the little boy. 'If you look at the picture, you'll see these big claws,' he said, his laser pointer highlighting the terrifying hooks. 'And black teeth.'

'You've created a terrifying miniature monster,' exclaimed Sophie, her eyes peering fearfully from between her fingers. 'But I don't get the point. Haven't you got anything better to do than invent a bionic flea?'

The professor wilted a little. 'Let me explain,' he said. 'This little creature . . .'

'Bob,' nodded Ollie.

'Is actually a tracking device. As we all know, GM451 has a tracker in her collar as well as one implanted under her skin, in her shoulder. So, worst case scenario, if any evil agents steal her, we can track her using this app,' he said holding up his mobile and showing a big red dot. 'She's here, right next to me,' he said. 'But these trackers are easy to detect. Anybody with half a brain would know that the collar has a tracker and someone with three-quarters of a brain would tell you that she has a microchip. Both are easily detected and removed. But a bionic flea? That's a game-changer. It uses its claws and teeth to hang on to canine hair. Almost invisible to the human eye and pretty much untrackable.'

'It's a good idea, Prof,' agreed Ben. 'But I don't see why Lara would need it. She's retired, remember? Lara, the pups and Shakespeare are family pets. We don't want any more adventures. Mum won't allow it,' he reminded him.

Lara looked at the children and her pups. Her head said that Ben was right but her heart yearned for adventure. The pups swished their tails as they remembered a recent mission in which they had saved the world from an evil baddy. Shakespeare sat on the table, his translating collar blinking away, taking it all in. He wasn't sure whether to agree with Ben or not.

Life as a family mog is awesome, but saving the world is rather exciting too.

'I understand what you're saying, young Benjamin,' said the professor, nodding, 'but you have to understand that GM451 has enemies. Retired or not, there may be evil villains plotting to dog-nap her. Or worse,' he said over the top of his glasses.

Sophie let out a small squeal and hugged her dog.

'And I don't want to panic anyone,' said the professor, lowering his voice and panicking everyone, 'but we've been picking up lots of internet chatter about strange goings-on in the criminal underworld.'

Lara cocked her head. 'What kind of goings-on, I wonder?' she woofed to Shakespeare.

'This is top secret stuff,' continued the scientist. 'We don't know who, or when, but we're picking up a very strong message about a kidnap plot. And,' he continued, lowering his voice to a whisper, 'there's been a spate of gunpowder thefts.' His eyes darted left and right, as if the thief might be in the room.

'Boom!' he exploded, making the children squeal and the cat's fur stand on end. 'Someone, somewhere is planning an explosion. So, GM451, if you'll allow me, I'd like to introduce you to, erm . . .'

'Bob,' nodded Ollie.

'Bob,' agreed the professor, bending down and unscrewing the lid. Nobody could see it, but Lara felt an itch as the bionic flea jumped aboard and made itself at home.

3. Record-Breaker

Mr Big had taken great care to secure the most secret 'secret lair' in the world. His men had spent months in the deepest part of the London underground, pretending to be maintenance staff, tunnelling twice as deep as the trains. The hideaway was 200 metres down and the walls lined with lead. He had rigged up a TV aerial but there was no chance of outside communications.

'If we can't hear them up there,' he snarled to his team, 'then they can't hear us down here.'

He was proud to be a record-breaker, reeling the statistics off to his team. 'Scariest human,' he began, 'three years on the bounce. Person least likely to be invited to a dinner party. Most crimes committed in a single day: that was two thousand and seventy-five,' he noted,

'quite a day. Biggest number of successful prison escapes . . . seven. Biggest bank robbery: papers said sixty-five mill but it was actually nearer seventy. The only person ever to escape Hurtmore Mega-Max Ultimate Security Prison, three times and counting,' he grinned. 'And, of course, the world's most wanted criminal. That's why I need deep cover,' he snarled, 'and two hundred metres is about as deep as you can go.'

The lair was a cross between a lounge, kitchen and classroom. Gus was sprawled in the lounge area, his huge body taking up most of the sofa. His boss described Gus as a throwback to olden times when criminals wore stockings over their heads and punched people. With a bald head, thick neck and vacant look, Gus was the kind of criminal who looked like a criminal, so Mr Big had been experimenting with a series of faces printed on his swanky 3D printer and the thug was currently wearing the face of his favourite female pop star.

Archie was a small, hairy man with darting eyes and a monobrow, almost a throwback to a time long before humans had properly evolved. Dark hair sprang out of the top of his Hawaiian shirt and his arms seemed extra-long. He was in the kitchen, peeling a banana.

Mr Big fiddled with the smartboard. 'Didn't have any of this when I was growing up.' He thought back to his school days, imagining how proud his teachers would be, knowing all that he'd achieved. At age nine he had already been an accomplished thief. *Small stuff, like lunch money and teachers' handbags. And then it just kind of mushroomed*, he thought, his chest swelling with pride at the memory of the time he'd stolen the head's car and sold it at lunchtime before returning to class to flash the cash. He chuckled to himself. *I was twelve and I thought that was the perfect crime, but little did I know that there were much bigger things to come.*

He remembered being asked the fateful question: 'What do you want to be when you grow up?' His school chums had trotted out the usual stuff; firefighter, astronaut and professional footballer. When it was his turn he'd said, 'Master criminal,' and while the teacher choked on his sandwich, Mr Big had gone on to explain that he wanted to be so brilliantly successful as a criminal that he'd be famous. 'A slebrity criminal,' he'd announced to the class.

He clapped his hands for attention. 'Gus, will you remove that ridiculous face,' he ordered. 'You look like a seven-foot schoolgirl.' The thug peeled off his fake face and revealed his standard ugly mug.

'So here we are, boys,' growled Mr Big to his trusted henchmen. 'Standing on the verge of being the most famous criminals the world has ever seen. This last crime will cement me into the all-time criminal hall of fame. And you guys will go down as my little helpers.'

'Like Santa's little helpers,' smiled Gus. 'Can we wear elf suits?'

'You'll be wearing my fist around your chops if you don't shut up,' growled the ringleader. 'Everybody has a dream, right, lads?' And while Gus's mind went to a Caribbean beach bar and Archie's head scuttled off to a treehouse in the forest, Mr Big was imagining chat shows and prime-time TV. *Strictly* maybe? He ran the show in his head, the one in which he swept one of the sequinned ladies off her feet with his Bolivian cha-cha before sweeping off with her diamond earrings. Or *Ultimate Prison Break?* He'd already written to the BBC with his idea for a reality TV show set inside. 'You choose the prison,' he'd written, 'and have a comp to see who can get out the quickest.' But, of all the programmes, he longed for his ultimate TV fantasy: Come Dine With Me*, in which I poison the other guests and make off with their laptops and cameras*. Come Die With Me *might be a better name for the show*, he thought.

Mr Big understood the power of TV. He figured there were celebrity chefs, celebrity scientists, celebrity YouTubers, celebrity antiques experts and loads of celebrity nobodies. So why not a celebrity criminal? But first he had to make the news.

'Boys, think back to all the famous criminals of the past. All those good guys that have gone before us. All those murderers and bank robbers.'

'Good guys? asked Gus. 'Like who, boss?'

'Like Dick Turpin, that's who to begin with,' snarled the ringleader. 'He was proper famous.

He was a highwayman who'd shout, 'Stand and deliver' and rob the rich folk. And there were the great train robbers who stole millions of quid from under the noses of the police. You see, boys, yer modern-day crook doesn't do classic crimes like that any more. It's all cyber this and internet that. It's all here today gone tomorrow crime. And most criminals are long forgotten.' He sucked hard on his cigar until his face turned grey. 'Except one,' he spat, the air turning blue with smoke. 'There's an all-time superhero villain who we've celebrated every year for four hundred years. An amazing guy. Literally!'

Archie and Gus looked confused.

'Amazing *Guy*?' he prompted. 'Guy Fawkes!' said their boss. 'Remember, remember the fifth of November? The bonfire? Fireworks?' He looked at Gus's blank face. 'Helloooo, anybody home?' he yelled, rapping his knuckles on the big man's skull.

'But isn't he famous for, like . . . failing?' asked Archie nervously. 'He was going to blow up the Houses of Parliament and got caught.'

'You can think of us as the modern day Guy Fawkes,' said Mr Big. 'Except we're not going to fail.'

'And we're not called Guy,' offered Gus, rubbing his sore head.

'Gentlemen, all you need to know is that we are going to outdo Mr Fawkes,' he said, his good eye gleaming as brightly as his glass one. 'Our crime will be celebrated for the next four hundred years.'

'We're gonna be rich,' shouted Gus, punching the air.

'Calm down, Gussy,' said his boss. 'We're already rich. Crime isn't always about the cash,' he said. 'Sometimes it's for the glory. Gentlemen, we are going to carry out a *successful* gunpowder plot. We're going to be more than rich. We're going to be famous. In fact,' he said, 'Archie, Google this for me . . . infamous.'

There was a moment's silence as Archie's fingers jabbed at the screen. 'Infamous,' he began. 'Adjective. Well known for some bad quality or deed.' He glanced at his boss who had closed his eyes. 'Wicked, abominable, unprincipled and unscrupulous.'

Mr Big's eyes remained closed and a small smile was etched across his face. 'Keep going.'

'Err, outrageous, shocking, disgraceful, monstrous . . .'

Gus leant over the iPad. 'Dreadful,' he smiled. 'Disgusting, terrible, loathsome. Boss, it's soooo you!'

Their boss sat for a few seconds, nodding silently. He opened his eyes and reached for a tissue, wiping away a tear of joy. 'Infamous, gentlemen, is what we're going to be.'

'Hence the plan,' said Archie, fidgeting in his chair, pulling his knees up to his chin, his long arms curling round his legs. 'So run us through it one more time, boss,' he said. 'I get it but I think the big lad might still be struggling.'

'Luckily,' said Mr Big, nodding, 'we're all playing to our strengths, so ape man here will be brute force and ignorance. I haven't given him a thinking part.'

The huge man beamed. 'Lots of hitting,' he guessed. 'And delivering,' he reminded himself. 'I'm driving the wagon.'

'You are indeed,' said Mr Big, pressing a key on his laptop. 'Here's the three-point plan, in reverse order. 'Number three: those barrels need delivering. One to every prison in England.'

Three pairs of eyes focused on the mass of barrels stacked in the corner of the room. 'With these handmade cards,' said Gus, wafting one above his head. He couldn't read, but he knew the squiggles said, 'Dear prison officers. Here's a barrel of free beer in celebration of all the fantastic work you've done this year. Please put it in your staffroom, but remember: not a drop until just after midnight on New Year's Eve. Lots of love, the Prime Minister.'

'And remind me of the detail?' prompted the ringleader.

'The detail is that I deliver one barrel of beer to every prison.'

'And . . .' said Mr Big, wrinkling his forehead and doing his encouraging hands.

'And . . . I must be very careful that when delivering the beer I don't get recognized. I am a wanted man. Not as wanted as you, boss.' He smiled. 'I mean like you're "most wantedest", but Archie and me, we're quite badly wanted too. So I'm fixing myself up with these glasses and this 3D face,' he said, wafting the disguise above his head.

'Yes,' grinned Mr Big. 'It's a masterpiece of a plan. You are visiting every prison, making a Christmas delivery. Who'd have thought that a quite badly wanted criminal would be breaking in, right in front of the officers' very noses?'

Mr Big clicked his laptop again. 'Number two,' he announced. 'Archie, remind me?'

'I'm a busy bee,' he whined. 'I've got a thinking part. I'm buzzing around recruiting lots of security guards. We've got thirteen hundred lined up, ready to start on the first of January. A small army of recruits, boss. Like you wanted. And I've got more interviews coming up, so we should have two thousand for when the time comes.'

Mr Big puffed on his cigar and inhaled deeply, pursing his lips and puffing out a perfect smoke ring. 'Will have,' he corrected. 'It's a beautiful plan, gentlemen. I mean, if it was a person, it would be a supermodel. Truly gorgeous.'

'I've been wondering though,' began Archie, his face twitching nervously. 'Like maybe why I'm recruiting security guards and like why Gus is delivering beer to the prison officers?'

Mr Big's smile faded, to be replaced by a scowl that left Archie regretting his question.

'Your job, chimp face, is not to wonder. I do the wondering. You and the missing link do the doing. If you get caught, you only know your bit so you can't confess to the whole crime. The coppers will never know what I'm up to. All you need to know is that it's the perfect crime and it's going to make a big noise. Gentlemen, we're going to pull off a crime that will make us the most notorious criminals of all time.'

'Slebrity criminals,' repeated Gus. 'It's all I ever wanted.'

Mr Big puffed another smoke ring, momentarily lost in thought as he pictured himself on a prime-time chat show. 'But of course, the plan starts with this.' He clicked the laptop once more to reveal the number one and a photo of a dog's face. It was a black and white dog with a sticky-up ear. 'Priority numero uno,' he snarled. 'Eliminate Spy Dog. And that, my primates, is going to be my pleasure.' He picked up a dart and hurled it at the smartboard, embedding the point between the dog's eyes.

Mr Big ground his cigar into the ashtray, blue smoke rising into his eyes. It was hot underground, but all of a sudden there was a chill in the air. 'GM451 is going to be GM six-feet-under.'

The Spy Dogs and Cat were in their office. Lara checked her watch. Six p.m. She raised her sticky-up ear and listened as the animals were arriving. 'It's time,' she woofed. 'Star, you stay here and watch the cameras while Spud and I go and run the pet neighbourhood watch meeting.'

Star wagged hard, proud to be in charge. 'I'll text you if anything comes in, Ma,' she woofed, making herself comfortable in the swivel chair.

Lara and Spud stood in the fireplace. Spud pressed the button and the fireplace rotated, swivelling the dogs into the lounge.

It was snowing so Lara had decided to hold the meeting in the kitchen. Dogs had been ordered to wipe their feet and Ned wasn't allowed in, so she'd opened a window and his long horsey head peered through over the sink. Lara looked round at the assembled animals – the neighbourhood's finest – mostly cats and dogs, with a few guinea pigs, a parrot, Syd the rat and, of course, Ned. George the tortoise had been excused because it was hibernating season, although Lara noted that he'd left strict instructions to be woken up if anything thrilling cracked off.

Lara was about to start the pet neighbourhood watch meeting when her mobile buzzed.

She glanced down. *People stealing flowers from the cemetery*, Star had texted.

Lara showed it to Spud. 'Sort this one for me, please,' she said, 'and take Lucy and Blake, in case you need some muscle.' The puppy nodded to the Alsatians and the three dogs bounded out of the meeting.

Lara rang a bell for attention and the animal chatter stopped. 'Welcome to the neighbourhood pet watch weekly update,' she woofed. Shake-speare was doing sign language for the cats, his paws working in double quick time. Lara waited until he was finished. 'We had a visit from the prof yesterday,' she announced. 'As well as intro-ducing us to some amazing new inventions, he also warned us that there might be a kidnap being plotted.'

There was a whoosh of animal chatter so Lara rang the bell again. Dessie the Dalmation was already on the worktop, peering out of the window. 'Down, Dessie,' ordered Lara. 'Not right here, right now. We don't even know who. But maybe sometime soon.'

Her mobile buzzed again. This time Star had written, *Shoplifting at the supermarket. 2 ladies. Urgent.* Lara glanced at the cats. 'Shakespeare,' she said, holding the message up for him to read, 'take the felines and go sort this.'

'On it,' mewed the ginger cat, taking five cat colleagues to help.

Lara looked at the assembled crowd, much smaller than it had been sixty seconds ago. 'The professor's information isn't clear cut. As you know, he has his ear to the criminal grapevine. He said it might be nothing more than internet chatter, but that we should be extra alert. First of all, there are rumours of a kidnapping plot . . .' Again Lara had to pause while the animals woofed and meowed excitedly. 'And,' she continued, 'the prof says several shipments of gunpowder have been stolen.'

'A gunpowder plot,' woofed Jasper. 'How thrilling. Or, erm, dangerous,' he corrected.

'So I'm stepping us up from level three, "eyes and ears alert", to level four, "noses too",' woofed Lara.

There was more commotion and Dessie was up again, this time sniffing the air. 'Down, boy,' sighed Lara, thinking this was more like a random bunch of pets than a crack animal neighbourhood watch team.

'Not again,' woofed Lara as the mobile buzzed a third time. 'Santa, Bruce and Jasper, can you run, or fly, whatever, down to the junior school. Star says there are some suspicious characters lurking around. We don't want anyone stealing the kids' computers. Maybe Ned will give you a lift.'

Six pets remained. 'We have cameras covering the town. And from our office we can watch like hawks . . .' Lara looked at Polly perched on the curtain rail, 'or parrots,' she corrected. 'All I'm asking is that we be extra vigilant in the next few days.'

'And what if we see or hear anything?' panted Marmaduke the bulldog.

'Or smell anything fishy,' wagged Dessie.

'You report direct to me,' reminded Lara. 'And we'll make a note and send you off to investigate.'

There was general agreement, the dogs wagging in excitement and the parrot and rat feeling mildly excited.

'So, let's revise what I just said, just to be sure that we all understand,' said Lara. She looked round the room. She eyed Dennis, the enthusiastic but not very bright Labrador. *If Dennis gets it, everyone will*, she thought.

Dennis stepped forward and puffed out his golden chest. 'To sniff out some fish and make notes,' he woofed.

Lara sighed. *That's not quite what I said*, she thought, *but that's as close as Dennis will ever get*. Lara was about to finish the meeting when Star burst into the kitchen.

'Ma,' she barked, 'the town's gone mad with crime. All of a sudden, there's so much cracking off.' She looked at her list. 'There's a man break-ing into a house on George Street and a drunken lady smashing windows and two youths break-ing into cars on the High Street. It's a crime wave, right on our doorstep. I've alerted the police.'

Lara blinked. 'Good work,' she woofed. 'The police will be coming from the city so they will take six minutes; meantime, let's allocate jobs to those in the room. Star, take these three to George Street. Dennis, do you know where the High Street is?'

The Labrador nodded. 'Is it the street where the butcher is?'

Lara nodded.

'I'm on it, boss,' he growled, taking the parrot and rat with him.

'Remember,' woofed Lara. 'Eyes, ears and noses alert.'

Lara looked round the empty kitchen. Her heart was racing and her mind felt a bit fuzzy. She felt uncomfortable.

Something's not right, she thought. She looked at the register. *Twenty-two pets summoned across town?* She tried to think straight.

The retired Spy Dog leafed through her

notebook, looking at the recorded crime figures for the year. February, one attempted shoplifting. September, one rather noisy party. Apart from that, nothing. And yet, here we are, with six crimes all happening at the same time. Before she had time to smell anything too fishy her thoughts were interrupted by the sound of a police siren.

'Phew, back-up,' she gasped. 'And quicker than six minutes. Well done, police.' The police van screamed up the cul-de-sac and screeched to a halt. A burly policeman jumped out and shouted to Lara.

'Quickly, Spy Dog; you're needed.' He threw open the back doors of his police van and Lara sprinted across the drive and hopped in. The back doors slammed and the man jumped into the driver's seat. 'Massive crime wave in the village,' he said, before sliding the glass partition shut.

The van lurched forward, Lara's senses dancing with excitement.

Eyes, ears and noses, she thought. Her eyes told her she was alone, locked in the back of a police van. *Not good*. Her ears could hear a faint hissing that she couldn't make out. Her nose sniffed something . . . *Not fishy, more gassy*, she thought. She looked through the glass partition at the back of the policeman's head. She tapped on the window.

'Hello,' she woofed. 'Can you let me out, please? I want to sit up front.' The man didn't look round. Lara's senses tightened. She tapped louder, this time more frantically. 'Hello,' she woofed. 'Officer, let me out, please.' The van sped forward, away from town and still the man didn't look round.

Lara's senses were on full alert and her mind was a jumble of thoughts that she tried to unravel. *A room full of pets, all called away at the same time. Rumours of a kidnap plot. But we don't know who, or when.*

Lara couldn't see the driver's face but she already knew. She dared to peer into the rear-view mirror and Mr Big's eyes stared back at her. She howled in anguish as he pressed a button and gas filled the back of the van. The last thing Lara remembered was seeing his evil eyes light up with glee.

4. Cliffhanger

Of the three-point plan, part three was going just fine. Gus's lorry was trundling up and down the motorways, delivering barrels of Home Office ale to every prison in the land.

Archie was in charge of part two. He now had 1,877 new security guards recruited, all due to start work on the first of January.

Part one was a dream. Mr Big had several mottos. 'If at first you don't succeed, kill someone,' was a good one, as was; 'A kind word costs nothing, but a very expensive rifle may prove more effective.' But there was one saying that he couldn't improve on; 'If you want a job doing properly, do it yourself,' so he had personally taken charge of part one, a task so crucial that he could trust nobody but himself. He'd recruited a small team to start a mini crime wave in the dog's village. He knew that would draw the dogs and cats away, leaving him free to dog-nap his black and white mongrel-faced enemy.

'Or GM451 or Spy Dog or whatever,' he snarled. He thought it was amusing that spy dog rhymed with die dog.

Lara awoke, her eyes blinking at the sky. Her head was throbbing and she couldn't move. She sniffed, her wet nose catching a strong sea smell, her ears confirming crashing waves somewhere very near. Her shoulder ached and she sniffed again. *Blood*.

Mr Big's evil face leered into view. 'You're awake,' he clapped. 'Welcome Die . . . I mean Spy Dog,' he chuckled, black tar churning up from his throat. He rolled some phlegm around his mouth and spat a black globule on the wet grass.

Lara was groggy. Her head was muzzled and her body stretched out, each leg pinned to the ground with a tent peg. The only thing she could move was her head. *Left, grass. Right, grass.* She arched her neck. *Behind, sea.* Lara put the pieces together and worked out that she was pegged out on a cliff, the sea crashing below.

And my arch enemy above! Lara remembered her first encounter with the man – the first of many – *in my Spy Dog days, before I'd met the kids, before I was a mum.* She was proud to have helped put him behind bars. *Which is where I thought he was now. Mega-max security? The world's most wanted? Why did nobody warn us he was on the outside?*

The leering face appeared again, this time with an even bigger grin. 'I like sayings,' he sneered. 'Like, 'Every dog has its day,' Well GM whatever-stupid-number-you-are, this is your day. Your *last* day,' he said, his cackle interrupted by another mouthful of smoker's cough.

Lara twisted her head and watched as he opened the van and picked up a baseball bat.

Not good, thought the retired spy, eyes every-where, senses alert. Lara was pegged, but she could feel that the peg pinning her left back leg was slightly loose. She flexed her thigh muscle and felt the peg loosen a bit more.

'So,' said Mr Big, this time prodding Lara's chest with the baseball bat, 'I thought we'd play a bit of sport.' He jabbed Lara more forcefully, and she winced. 'Bat and ball.' He produced a bloody knife. 'I have removed your tracker,' he said, 'so it's just you and me, with no prying eyes. But before we play I thought I'd let you into my little secret.'

Lara blinked as drizzle began to fall into her eyes. She flexed a bit more and felt the peg loosen. She knew she had less than half a chance. *But it's all I've got*.

'Me and my gang have got a plan. Let's call it a gunpowder plot. We've delivered a barrel of beer to every prison in the country. Gus has literally broken into every prison, right under the noses of the officers. I think you'll agree, Die Dog, that's quite a daring mission. Except it's not beer, it's gunpowder, and when Big Ben strikes midnight, every barrel will go bang.' He prodded Lara's chest again, this time very hard, taking her breath away.

Lara's left leg twitched. She was ready to wriggle, but her other legs felt securely pegged down, so she doubted she could escape.

'So every prison wall will have a dirty great hole in it. And every dangerous criminal will escape. The country will be flooded with the worst of the worst. Let me tell you, Die Dog, these are people you really wouldn't want to meet in a dark alley.'

People like you, thought Lara, straining at the ropes.

'And citizens will need to feel safe. With so many evil crims on the loose the police will be overwhelmed. People will need security guards. And who do you think has the biggest army of security guards, ready to start work on the first of January?'

Mr Big paused for a second, smiling into the

middle distance as he considered changing his middle name. He'd never liked Colin. *Something double-barrelled, maybe, that would sound good on TV. Something like Evil Genius perhaps? Or Infamous?*

'So, with one week to go, what's a villain to do? You keep stopping my cunning plans so I thought it'd be best if you weren't around.' Mr Big raised the bat above his head. 'Goodnight, old girl. Sweet dreams.' The bat came down very hard indeed.

Lara's left leg yanked the peg out of the ground and she managed to twist her body to avoid the full blow. The bat caught the side of her head and she saw stars. Dazed, Lara yanked at the ropes and the pegs pinning her other legs came loose. She staggered as the bat came down again, this time catching her right shoulder. Lara fell to the ground and the bat came down with massive force on her spine. *Oof.* The rain was pouring now. She heard Mr Big spit again. *And he's laughing. He's actually enjoying hurting me.* There was no time to think. *Just trust your instincts.* Lara rolled sideways and swirled her right front leg, *My good leg*, with the rope and tent peg still attached. She lassooed Mr Big's legs and he came down, face first, into the grass.

Lara felt helpless. *My best weapons – my teeth – are muzzled*. She knew she couldn't run. Blood was running down her face, her front left leg was limp and her head was buzzing with a loud noise. She watched in frustration as the man righted himself.

'I like it that you fight to the bitter end,' he said, almost admiringly. 'And bitter it is going to be.'

The man walked forward, slapping the baseball bat in his hand. Lara inched backwards, the noise in her head hurting more than her limp leg. *At least two cracked ribs*, she thought. The muzzle was stopping her barking, but she could still do a terrifying growl. The stricken dog reached the edge of the cliff and the man kept coming. The bat was now in two hands, to give a bigger blow. Lara knew that she couldn't take any more. Her face was swollen, her left eye closed.

Good eye forward, her legs probed behind and she felt the cliff edge with her feet. She daren't look down. The ocean roared below. He came again and Lara dodged, snarling and kicking. The last blow was a swipe that caught Lara on the side of the head. She could see two of him. Lara's back legs slipped and she fell. He kicked her face and she felt blood in her mouth. The dog staggered backwards, but there was nowhere to go. She winced in agony as her good back leg scrabbled for a hold and her front paws clung to the cliff.

Lara looked up at Mr Big. *Two of him, both grinning*. Her back legs were still scrambling for a foothold as she dangled from the cliff. The man stamped on her right paw, but she refused to yelp. Dangling by one paw, Lara couldn't hold on much longer. She didn't wait for him to stamp again. *I won't give him the satisfaction*. Lara closed her eyes, a lifetime of adventures screaming through her mind.

She let go and fell backwards, her legs flailing and her eyes fixed on the smiling criminal.

Mr Big's hands were shaking as he lit another cigar. He stood for a while, leaning over the cliff, savouring a moment of evil pleasure. He puffed hard as he watched waves crashing on to the rocks below, until he was satisfied that there was no dog. The criminal flicked the end of his cigar.

'Ashes to ashes, and all that,' he growled, stamping the ash into the wet turf with his foot.

'With spy-poochy out of the way, nothing can stop my gunpowder plot.'

The bionic flea was dazed. Lara had been hit with such force that its claws had become loose and it had bounced off the dog into the wet grass. Bob's software analysed his surroundings and didn't like them one bit. His habitat was hair, not grass. He jumped once, his tiny camera assessing the situation. He ran his surroundings through his information processor once more. A sheep eighty metres away. Or a hairy human ankle, two metres. *Boink*. Bob leapt on to Mr Big's ankle and nestled into the hairs.

Mr Big turned and lumbered back to the van. It hadn't quite gone to plan, but he was sure the dog was gone. He turned the key and pulled the seatbelt across his chest, scratching his ankle as he drove the van away.

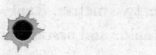

5. Unhappy Christmas

The professor and children met Star, Spud and Shakespeare. The animals held their heads in shame. They knew they'd fallen for the oldest trick in the book; what the professor called 'chaos and distraction'.

'Don't hold yourselves responsible,' he said. 'Somebody set up that mini crime wave to get GM451 isolated. It could have happened to any of us.'

'It's been twenty-four hours, Professor,' said Ben. 'Where on earth can she be? And, more to the point, who has taken her and why?'

'That second bit, I'm not sure,' admitted the scientist. 'But the where is a bit easier.' He held up his mobile phone. 'The bionic flea app is signalling from two hundred miles away on the south coast.'

'Yey, Bob's alive and well,' sang Ollie, punching the air and then bouncing round the room like a flea.

The professor's face told a different story. 'So the pups and myself got a copter down there and did a bit of sniffing around, so to speak. Obviously, it was canine agents that did the sniffing. You see, if I had done it, it would have looked rather strange. Besides, humans don't have such a good sense of –'

'What did you find, Professor?' cut in Sophie.

'Yes, well . . . the pups sniffed that GM451 had been there. They were very worried that they could smell blood. It was all at the cliff edge you see.'

Sophie's hand went to her mouth and she stifled a scream.

'Agent Spud found some tyre tracks and another clue, some rope. But the flea trail has gone quiet,' admitted the scientist. 'Bob's gone off grid,' he whimpered, his voice breaking with emotion. 'It must have broken or run out of battery life, or something. Wherever she is, I'm afraid GM451 is on her own.'

Ben was trying his best to keep a brave face, but Sophie and Ollie were crying as the professor ushered them into a taxi and sent them home. He returned to his laboratory, tears welling in his eyes. He stood alone.

'What's the point in inventing if all my inventions go wrong?' he muttered to himself, 'and I lose the animal I love the most?' His laboratory was quiet, the Bunsen burners off and the classical music gone. The scientist took a seat and rocked gently in his chair, glasses off, eyes focused on blurriness. He picked up his phone and held it close-up, checking the flea app one more time.

'Nothing!' He threw the device towards the sink. It hit the wall and plopped into the water. 'Useless. Even underwater because you can't even speak underwater. What an idiot. Everything is useless. And I'm the most useless thing of all,' he sobbed.

It had been the worst Christmas ever. Mum and Dad were upset, Ben hadn't opened a single present, Sophie was puffy-faced and even Ollie had seemed sad. Spud had managed a wag at turkey time, but that was the only sign of happiness. So, on Boxing Day, Dad loaded the children into the car. 'Mystery tour,' he

beamed. 'I know just the thing to cheer you all up. One condition, blindfolds on for this special Christmas surprise.'

The kids sat in silence, scarves around their heads, with Dad singing karaoke-style to his 'best Xmas in the universe ever' hits.

'No peeking,' he said as the kids stumbled out of the car. 'Up this step, into this room and *ta-daaaa:* blindfolds away!'

The children pulled their scarves off. They were outside an RSPCA home. Sophie started sobbing and her little brother gave her a hug. Ben looked at the six dogs and shook his head. 'Dad, how could you?' he began, his voice cracking with emotion.

'You choose.' Dad smiled. 'Lara was your dog really, son. I've narrowed it down to these six. There's even a black and white one,' he said. 'You know, in case you wanted one the same.'

'I don't want one *the same*,' said the boy glaring at his dad. 'I want "the one". The one and only. The best dog in the world.' His eyes welled over. 'I want my best friend back.'

The six dogs wagged as Ben turned on his heel and slammed the door.

'I'll walk home,' he shouted.

Bob the flea had had a very busy Christmas. He'd migrated across Mr Big's ankle and then followed the hair trail up his leg, along his hairy bum crack, through his chest hair and settled in a nice tuft behind his ear. The man kept scratching and Bob noticed he had begun to use anti-dandruff shampoo. But Professor Cortex had built a sturdy flea and his miniature claws clung on, even in the shower.

It wasn't the bionic flea's fault that he was 200 metres underneath London. His transmissions were bouncing round the lead-lined walls. Mr Big had assembled Archie and Gus for a celebration. He popped a bottle of bubbly and grinned so widely that his plastic-surgeoned face almost cracked.

'Gentlemen,' he said, gold teeth glinting, 'we are actually ahead of time.' He poured fizz into the glasses, and each frothed over. 'Part three, Gus, remind me?'

'Err, my bit is done, boss,' he said. 'Barrels delivered to every prison, with a note from the prime minister. 'And,' he added, 'one barrel left over, just as you said there would be.' The three men looked at the barrel propping the door open, HOME OFFICE ALE emblazoned on the side.

'Part two, Archie?'

'My bit's gone very well too, boss,' sang Archie in his whiny voice. 'You wanted 2,000 security guards and I've only gone and gotcha 2,003.'

Mr Big nodded his approval. 'So let's raise our glasses to part one,' he suggested, raising his own glass in the air and watching the bubbles rise to the top. 'To a dear departed

mutt. Man's best friend is now man's dead friend. To a dead Spy Dog.'

'To a dead Spy Dog,' chorused his henchmen. Mr Big sank his champagne in one large gulp, as he scratched behind his ear. 'Now to part four,' he announced, 'the gunpowder plot.'

6. The Fight

The dog woke. There was a loud humming in her head and her side ached.

Probably broken ribs, she thought. She was lying on a beach, waves pulling at her body. She heaved herself into a sitting position, the effort nearly making her black out. *I'm shaking.* She was muzzled and had ropes tied to her front legs. Her vision was blurry. The dog's first attempt to stand failed, her back legs giving way. It was a full ten minutes before she had summoned enough strength to limp up the beach, out of reach of even the biggest waves.

She noticed that the noise of the ocean was drowned out by the siren in her head. *Not good.* The dog caught sight of herself in a rock pool. *How odd.* She saw that she was black and white with a sticky-up ear. The left side of her face

71

was swollen and both eyes were bloodshot. *Not a pretty sight*, she thought. *Looks like I've been roughed up. But by whom?*

The dog spent a few minutes rubbing against a sharp rock to sever the ropes round her legs. *Why was I tied up? And why was I in the sea? And who am I?*

She tugged at her muzzle until the restraint worked loose, then she limped along the beach towards a town.

Maybe I'll find some answers there, she thought. The grey December day summed up the town.

Past its best, thought the dog. She noticed there were a few Christmas lights rattling from the lamp posts in a half-hearted attempt to bring some festive cheer. Her body was weak, but her brain was functioning. She looked through the window of one of the houses. *Christmas tree with dropping needles*, she noticed. *Probably after Christmas and almost New Year*. The dog reckoned 30 December and, by the angle of the sun, 8.30 a.m. *Chalk cliffs, so south coast of England*. She watched as a man came out of a cafe and threw a half-eaten bacon roll into the bin. The dog waited until the coast was clear before rummaging in the bin and retrieving the meal, wolfing it hungrily.

Needed ketchup, she thought, *but not bad*.

The buzzing in her head was stopping her thinking straight. Images flashed across her mind.

But they make no sense. A boy. A grinning face. An evil one. A baseball bat.

She shook her head, trying to rid herself of the images. She limped on. The town was quiet. *Battened down for the winter months*, she thought. All of a sudden there was a yowl and a ginger cat sprang across the road and into a garden, its hair fluffed in terror.

The dog watched, more weird memories flooding her brain. *Ginger cat?* That image led to a little girl. *And an older boy?* A few seconds later three huge dogs sprinted across the road, a car horn beeping at the near miss. The black and white dog watched as the cat sank its claws into a tree and clambered on to a branch. It stood, back arched, hissing and spitting at the dogs below.

The three dogs barked, until one of them ordered, 'Cool it, guys. We don't want to draw attention to ourselves. We can wait. The mog will have to come down sooner or later.' The biggest of the three looked up at the hissing cat. 'You can run, pusskins, but you can't hide. Not from Razor and the gang.'

The black and white dog watched for a few minutes. Whenever the ginger cat attempted to come down the tree, the dogs barked in fury, threatening to tear the puss apart.

The dog wasn't sure who she was, but she knew what she stood for.

I hate injustice, she thought. *And bullying*. She

limped across the road and through the garden gate. The three larger dogs eyed her. 'Crikey, girl, did you run into a tree? Your face is a horror. You coming to help us deal with this cat?'

She continued to limp forward. 'No, guys,' she woofed, 'I'm coming to make sure you don't do the puss any harm. Three against one? Doesn't seem fair to me. Smacks of bullying and I hate bullies.'

The dogs looked momentarily confused before the pack leader broke into a howl of laughter. 'Nice one, sister. Very funny.'

The black and white dog didn't look amused. She continued to edge forward, her mind racing. *Three dogs, all bigger than me. Healthy, well fed, so very strong. But Rottweilers are slow. Never fight unless you have to*, she remembered from somewhere. *Use your brain first and combat powers for emergencies only.*

'Lads,' she said, 'why don't you back off and go and find something productive to do? Help an old lady cross the road or bark at a burglar, maybe? Do something good for the canine species.'

'Are you for real?' barked the pack leader.

'Razor, I presume?' she woofed, wishing she could remember her own name. 'Oh, I'm very real,' woofed the black and white dog, sounding more confident than she felt. Her blood was racing and the noise in her head was pounding louder with every heartbeat.

The atmosphere changed in an instant as the pack leader lowered his voice to a growl. 'What right have you got to come into our neighbourhood and lay down the law?' he warned. 'Three dogs to one cat? How about three dogs to one dog? Or,' he growled, confidence rising in his throat, 'six of us.'

The black and white dog turned her head to see three more of Razor's gang coming up from the rear. Hackles were raised as the dogs surrounded her. She had no idea where the plan came from, but she instinctively stood on her hind legs, her left one screaming in pain. Her eyes darted left and right and she tested the springiness of her legs, wincing in pain as she bounced up and down a couple of times. *Fifty per cent fit, at best*, she calculated. *The odds aren't terrific.*

'Get her,' ordered Razor.

One of the dogs at the rear was a bull mastiff. *Faster than the others*, calculated the dog. She kicked out behind and caught the dog in its privates. She didn't see it but she heard the yowl. *Eyes forward*, she caught Razor with a left jab, right on the chin. He staggered. She pulled her elbow down on top of the head of another dog and he was out cold. She sidestepped and two of the slower dogs collided. The leader was coming again. *This time from two o'clock*. The black and white dog knew it would hurt, but she kicked out with her bad leg and caught him in the mouth, leaving his three top teeth glistening in the grass. She swivel-kicked an attacker in the chin, knocking him unconscious too. She was still upright, springing on her toes. *Who's next?*

Another came at her from behind and she yelped as his claws scratched down her side. Quick as a flash she spun, landing an uppercut to his left eye. *Boom.* And a sharp jab to the chin. She assessed the situation. The blur of fur had been stopped. Four dogs lay in a heap. *Two are still in the game.*

The toothless leader could taste his own blood. He'd never been so angry, or afraid, so he went in again, this time head down, using brute force. It was a good plan. He caught the black and white dog in the stomach, knocking the air out of her. *Ooof.*

Her already sore ribs were now almost certainly broken and her breathing was painful. She got back to her feet and he came with one last charge. His head met an expert kick-boxer paw and his bottom teeth tinkled on to the patio.

The black and white dog stood tall, bouncing on her hind legs, trying to mask the agony she was in. Her front paws were circling, martial arts style. Her mind was ablaze with memories of fighting. She remembered being awarded her black belt and the picture in her mind was of a white-coated old man.

Who's he? she thought.

The pack leader's mouth was pouring blood and the side of his face was swollen. She noticed that his eyes were angry. *But there's fear too — rightly so*, she thought as she looked around at the four unconscious gang members. Razor's remaining friend was backing off and she sensed the fight was done.

'There's more if you want it,' she barked, shadow boxing.

'It'th not right,' woofed the dog through a toothless mouth. 'Protectin cath. You're a dog.'

'I'm a dog,' she heard herself saying, 'but I'm not a bully.' She felt herself standing tall, despite the pain, her chest out in a superhero pose. 'I stand for truth, justice and all that's right.' *Crikey where did that come from?* she thought. *But it seems to have worked.* The two remaining dogs slunk away.

The ginger cat clawed his way down the tree and threw himself at Lara in a furry hug. 'My hero!' he meowed. 'You saved my life. That was the bravest thing I've ever seen.'

The black and white dog wasn't sure what to do. Images queued up in her head, moving so fast that she couldn't concentrate. *A ginger cat called Shakespeare. A little girl. A man with a gun.* She put her paw to her ear and felt the bullet hole. *That leering face again. A man in a white coat. What does it all mean?* The cat held on, burying himself in the dog's tummy. The dog hugged back.

'You're like some sort of ninja dog,' meowed the puss. 'Like a superhero.'

The black and white dog was confused. Her brain ran more images. *Tunnels, gold, guns and a terrifying falling feeling, from a rocket?* She had no idea that the random pictures were memories.

And then a number came to her.

What on earth does GM451 mean? she wondered.

7. Checking In

The black and white dog wasn't quite sure why she felt so sad, *but I do*. She ached all over but that was nothing compared to the pain in her heart. *Like a missing piece*. The more she tried to think, the louder the ringing in her head. It helped when she relaxed – the images and sounds rushing into her mind became a little clearer. Above all, a boy kept appearing. *Always smiling*, she thought, the image in her head staying still just long enough for her to get a good look. *But who is he and where is he? And why do I miss him so much?*

The dog had found an abandoned warehouse. *I need some rest*, she thought as she flopped on to the cold stone floor and lay, her nose on her feet. *I've just taken out six burly dogs. I did karate on them. I don't think that's normal canine behaviour.* Her eyes closed, her mind relaxed and the images became stronger. *Benjamin?* she thought. But the image shifted and she was being hit with a baseball bat. *That leering face. And a plan about Big Ben?* And then she was in a deep sleep, falling off a cliff, legs flailing . . .

The dog woke with a start. There was a man in front of her. She tried to jump to her feet, her broken ribs causing her to yelp in pain. Before she could move, the man took a pole with a noose and expertly looped it round her neck. She tried to make herself heavy and fought all the way, but she was powerless to stop him. She noted that the van had *Dog Rescue* written on the side. She was ushered inside and the doors slammed shut. The driver jumped in.

'Local mutt centre is full of unwanted Christmas dogs,' he announced to himself. 'So me and you, girl, are taking a trip to London. Battersea Dogs Home, here we come.'

The black and white dog had decided to go quietly. *I wanted to go to London anyway, to check out the Big Ben thing.* She allowed the man to put a lead on her and she limped by his side into the Battersea Dogs and Cats Home office.

'Another one for doggy daycare,' smiled the man. 'A stray from down south,' he explained. 'A bit battered,' he said, 'no doubt been beaten up by the local dogs. They're a rough lot.'

I beg your pardon, thought the stray. *I might not be able to remember much, but I can remember this morning's little escapade. I think you'll find it was six against one, and the six got a walloping.*

'And not much of a looker,' said the man. 'Check the ear arrangement.'

The lady laughed. 'One sticky-up ear,' she noted. 'With a hole. How very strange. Anyway, Roy, leave her with us and we'll get her cleaned up and see if we can find her a nice home.' The lady clicked a camera and the dog's eyes blurred as the flash went off. 'For the internet, doggie,' she said. 'But it might be a while before you're adopted because our customers tend to go for the pretty dogs.'

The dog glared. *Harsh*, she thought, *although I do look a little worse for wear.* The lady led the black and white mongrel into the yard where 212 dogs were barking and jumping up and down at the bars. *More memories*, thought the dog as she remembered being caged. *And chosen?* The face of Benjamin appeared again and for the first time since waking up on the beach, she felt a wag in her tail.

Whoever he is, maybe he works here, she thought, eyes darting and sticky-up ear pricked. *Seven members of staff currently on duty*, she noted. The dog looked at a staff rota on the wall, *and another seven scheduled in. None called Benjamin.* She glanced at the name badge of the lady who was walking her. *Jennifer. Bad shoes, but by the smell of her she's got two dogs of her own at home.* She sniffed again and studied the strands of hair on her jumper. *Boxer and a terrier. And two bunches of keys jangling in her left pocket.* The dog trotted alongside the lady, taking a closer look. *One set of house keys and another bunch of dog-kennel keys.*

There was wild barking from the inmates as the new dog was checked in. 'You're doomed,' she heard one of them bark. 'I've been here for a year. Once you're in, there's no way out.' The black and white dog laughed to herself – *as if* – as she trotted alongside Jennifer. The lady removed the kennel keys from her pocket and studied them. She found the one she wanted and inserted it into the keyhole of cage number 451.

'Meet Trixie and Beyoncé,' said the woman, as she unlocked the door and shoved the new dog in. 'Be nice, ladies. Oh, and enjoy your stay.' She clicked the door shut and left them to make friends.

The newcomer's head was swirling. *Cage number 451?* The dogs sniffed each other. 'Hi there,' woofed the poodle. 'I'm Trixie. What's your name?'

'My name?' her face creased as a jumble of memories came flooding back. She saw a white-coated man. *Professor Cortex*, she remembered. 'I'm . . . GM451,' woofed the new dog, unsure where that had come from.

'That's one weird name,' woofed Beyoncé.

The black and white dog was overcome with exhaustion. She retreated to the back of the kennel and slumped to the floor.

It is a weird name, she thought. Tomorrow was New Year's Eve. *And I can't get Big Ben out of my head. Or little Ben come to think of it.* She closed her eyes and a movie of memories started playing in her mind. She let them come. *GM451? Or Lara?* she thought. *And I have Star and Spud.* It was all becoming clearer. She knew she needed to rest. *Something in the back of my*

mind tells me tomorrow is going to be a big day. She decided to stay for one night. Her eyes closed and she fell into a deep sleep, her body twitching and her mind slotting memories back into their rightful place.

Mr Big had spent Christmas alone in his underground lair. His scalp was red and unbearably itchy which meant he had to go upstairs. This was his first trip into daylight for six days, so he was ultra-cautious. He climbed the ladder, crawled through the tunnel and up another ladder. He stopped at the small hole in the wall and listened. The coast was clear, so he hauled himself through to the other side. *Always a tight squeeze*. He was in the London Underground, Northern Line, ladies' toilet, cubicle number six. He replaced the NOW WASH YOUR HANDS sign so that it covered his hidey-hole. Mr Big dusted himself down, flushed the toilet and prepared himself for what was always an awkward moment. *Deep breath!* He opened the door.

'Morning, miss,' he said to the lady applying her lipstick, before joining the crowds.

Mr Big glanced up at the security camera and pulled his hat down as far as it would go. He assumed his dark shades in December would be judged as a fashion statement rather than a disguise. He stood on the right of the escalator and then, collar up, he emerged on the busy street. Eyes down, he battled through the throng of shoppers.

Just need to nip in here, he thought, darting into a chemist's shop for some itchy scalp shampoo. *That other stuff just isn't working*. He beeped his purchase through the self-service checkout.

The criminal joined the pavement traffic again, head down but eyes alert. He'd enjoyed his brief glimpse upstairs but he was taking no chances. Mr Big scratched behind his ear as

he retraced his steps back down to his lair, emergency anti-dandruff shampoo safely purchased.

Bob had also enjoyed the trip upstairs. The bionic flea had used the sunshine to recharge his battery. The trip had been brief, but Bob was sure that he was now emitting a strong signal.

Professor Cortex had also spent Christmas alone. He'd normally have had dinner with the Cooks, exchanging presents, pulling crackers and sharing their turkey. He looked at the screen saver on his computer – *last Christmas*, he remembered. His silly grin beamed out of the screen. *My paper hat is a bit squiffy but look at GM451's.* He smiled to himself. *And Spud had attached a bauble to the hole in her sticky-up ear. Happy days indeed.* The professor looked away. He couldn't take it. His eyes looked round the deserted laboratory.

'It's pointless. Everything I worked for . . . it's not here,' he said aloud. 'It was there. In that moment.' The mild-mannered scientist felt rage welling up inside. 'GM451 – she wasn't just a dog,' he shouted, sweeping some glass jars off the worktop with his arm. His feet crunched on the broken glass, his rage building.

'She wasn't even *just* a spy. She was the best thing that ever happened to me,' he yelled, the vein on his forehead throbbing angrily. He picked up a crate of test tubes and threw them across the room, shards of glass tinkling everywhere. He looked at his screen saver again, another picture rotating into position; this one was a terrible selfie he'd taken last summer, with Ben, Sophie, Ollie and Lara with ridiculous grins, all dressed in white lab coats.

'Bring your family to work day,' he sobbed. 'The best day of my life.' He picked up his coffee cup and hurled it at the wall. A black stain appeared above the sink, the mug making a hollow cracking sound as it exploded.

He sat and sobbed for a full ten minutes while loneliness and sadness worked their way out through his tears. Eventually he sniffed, took a deep breath and stood up. The tears had washed away the doubt. His eyes were blurry but his head was clear.

'I can't just give up on GM451,' he said to himself. 'I've been totally selfish. If the roles were reversed, she wouldn't give up on me.'

He crunched across the broken glass to the cupboard and pulled out a brush and dustpan.

He began to sweep furiously – *a tidy room is a tidy mind* – until, 'Ouch!' the professor cut his finger on the broken glass. The old man stuck his finger in his mouth to stem the bleeding. He rushed over to the sink and turned the cold tap on. As red water filled the sink he noticed the mobile phone, still underwater where he'd thrown it ten days ago. Through the ripples he could see the flea app was flashing.

'No way!' The professor plunged his bloodied hand into the icy water and pulled out the mobile. He started to jump round the laboratory like a flea. 'Bob's alive, he's actually alive.' He wrapped a paper towel around his cut finger.

'No, no,' he reminded himself, 'Bob's a gadget. He's a tiny machine. GM451 is alive.' He tapped the screen and a map of central London appeared, a blue dot pulsating. 'And I'm going to rescue her.'

8. The Journey

It was the morning of New Year's Eve. Mum and Dad had gone to visit Aunty Brenda, leaving Ben in charge. He'd set up his bedroom as mission control, like he'd seen on TV police dramas, with clues pinned on the wall. There was a picture of Lara in the middle of the wall – Ben's favourite, his dog with a party hat on. To Lara's right was a postcard of some white cliffs with a big arrow pointing to a spot that said LAST KNOWN SIGHTING. To the left was a Post-it note that said BOB NOT WORKING and TYRE TRACKS AT SCENE.

'It was Shakespeare who found it,' said Sophie. 'He's such a clever puss. And it's only a rumour but, if you think about it, it makes perfect sense.'

The cat stretched with pride. 'Puuuurfect,' he purred.

'In her role as Spy Dog, Lara caught so many criminals, right? So we made a list from this file,' said Sophie, holding up a bulging folder. 'And there was one name that kept cropping up.'

'Mr Big?' guessed Ben. 'They were like arch-enemies. She caught him six times. He hates her. And she loathes him.'

'And he escaped five times,' said Sophie. 'From the most maximum security prisons.'

'And he's in Hurtmore Prison right now,' said Ben. 'What did they call it? Some special kind of security that was invented just for him? Ultra max?'

'Mega-Max Ultimate Security,' read Sophie from the file. 'The world's most dangerous criminal was in solitary confinement in the hyper-max wing. With a face mask and chained up, twenty-three hours and fifty-five minutes a day.'

'Was?' noted Ben, looking alarmed.

'Well,' said his sister looking at her notes, 'we contacted the prison governor to ask about Mr Big and she was really shifty. Wouldn't give us a straight answer. When we asked about the twenty-three hours and fifty-five minutes thing, she got really nervous. She asked us what we knew about the five minutes that he wasn't chained.'

'And?' asked her brother, half afraid of the answer.

'And pusskins here trawled the dark internet and the chatter is that Mr Big has escaped. Again! But that nobody's supposed to know because if the news got out there'd be panic and everything. So, we can't absolutely confirm it,' said the girl gravely, 'and we've no idea how, but we think he might have got out again.'

Her big brother was nodding. 'That's it,' he said. 'Makes perfect sense. He took Sophie's picture of the evil man and pinned it to the wall. 'But how on earth do we find Big and Lara?'

The silence was broken by the patter of tiny paws galloping up the stairs. Star ran in, a piece of paper in her mouth. Spud arrived a few seconds later, tongue lolling and eyes wide. 'We've found her,' woofed Star. 'We've been searching vets and animal rescue centres. Mum, she's alive!'

'What on earth are you two so excited

about?' asked Ben. 'Quit your yapping, we're trying to concentrate. We think Mr Big might be involved and we're trying to suss out where Lara might be.'

Star spat the piece of paper out of her mouth and set to work trying to unfold it with her paws. 'Ben, help me,' she whined, nosing his hand. 'Quickly. I've just printed this off.'

The boy took the paper. 'What have you got for me, pup?' he asked, unfolding the piece of A4.

'What is it?' asked his sister, watching as his eyes grew wide and his mouth dropped open. 'You look like you've seen a ghost.'

Ben turned the piece of paper so his sister and brother could see. Lara's battered and swollen face stared out from the paper. Sophie squealed, partly in delight and partly because her pet looked so beaten. 'It says she's been taken in by Battersea Dogs Home.'

'That's in London,' said Ben. 'Team, pack your bags. I'll get on the internet and buy some tickets – we've got a train to catch.' He knew Mum would go mad when she found out he'd borrowed her credit card, but it was a price worth paying. He clicked BUY and noted the reference number. 'We pick the tickets up from a machine at the station,' he said. 'Ready?'

'Ready,' chanted his brother and sister together.

'Ready,' woofed Ben and Ollie's backpacks.

'Let's go,' meowed Sophie's.

Ben and his posse marched off, chatting on the way. 'If we told Mum and Dad that Mr Big had escaped and dog-napped Lara, they'd either not believe us or just call the police, and what good would that do?' said Ben. 'It was the authorities that let him out in the first place.'

'And Mum and Dad don't get it,' agreed Sophie. 'They think that just getting another dog will make everything all right.'

The machine spat out three tickets and the children had no trouble boarding the train to St Pancras. The ticket inspector gave them a suspicious look, but she knew that children never ran away in a group – they were always alone. 'Going to London?' She smiled as she clipped their tickets.

'Yes,' said Ollie, 'our Spy Dog's been dog-napped by an evil baddie. Well, more than evil. Like . . .' he looked at his sister, 'what's beyond evil, Sof?'

'A nasty villain who wants to destroy the world,' she bellowed, unaware that her earphones were making her shouty. The carriage went quiet.

'Yes, that,' said Ollie. 'And we're going to save her. From the dogs' home.'

The lady smiled. 'Sounds very exciting,' she said, before moving on to the next passengers.

The children and animals arrived at St Pancras station. 'We're here, pups,' whispered Ben as they made their way through the crowded station. 'Stay hidden until we reach the outside.'

The children sat in St Pancras Square and opened their backpacks. Three furry animals jumped out. 'Phew, it was hot in there,' woofed Star.

'And I'm starving,' said Spud, sniffing a nearby McDonald's. 'Being smuggled on a train doesn't half make you hungry.'

Ben rummaged for his phone. He clicked on Google maps and the blue dot appeared. 'That-a-way,' said Ben pointing towards the river.

'Battersea Dogs Home and my Lara. We need to rescue Lara and then we might be able to see the fireworks at midnight. It'll be a great way to celebrate. I've seen them on telly,' said Ben, remembering last year, when he'd been allowed to stay up until midnight. 'There are massive fireworks in all the world's major cities at midnight. Usually starts with Sydney I think. And then it's London and New York. Big Ben strikes midnight and *boom*,' he said. 'It's an amazing sight.'

Mr Big was putting the final touches to this year's spectacle. 'Even more amazing than usual,' he smirked. A huge picture of Big Ben was beamed on to the smartboard. 'The target,' he said. 'The most famous clock in the world.'

'Big Ben,' nodded Gus, proud that he knew something.

Mr Big felt a little irritated but decided to carry on. Most people knew that it was actually the bell that was called Big Ben. The clock was just a clock in the Elizabeth Tower. But Gus wasn't most people. He was of limited intelligence, so explaining this would just take too long. He'd already had to explain the saying 'bold as brass' to Gus.

'We've got perfect fake ID,' he said. 'The

real clock maintenance team are tied up in their workshop. We've got their van, their outfits, tools, etcetera. So at eleven p.m. tonight we will turn up . . .'

Gus smiled. 'Bold as brass.'

His boss nodded politely. 'And Big Ben gets looked at on New Year's Eve every year so nobody will suspect a thing. What I've learned as the world's most successful criminal is this,' he began. 'First of all, the golden rule . . .'

'Don't get caught?' suggested Archie.

'Apart from that,' said their boss. 'It's amazing what you can get away with, under people's noses, if you look confident.' He pointed to the photo. 'We're going to pull up outside the Houses of Parliament . . .

'The highest-security building in the whole of London,' grinned Archie.

'As you can see from the picture, the clock tower is attached to the Houses of Parliament. That door is the only way into the clock tower. We will flash our passes and gain entry. Once in, the guards will lead us to the clock tower and leave us to it.'

'And that's when Archie does his big bang theory,' smiled Gus.

'It's no theory, Gussie me lad,' purred the mastermind. 'It's a very practical thing that is going to result in a lot of attention and money for me.'

'Which you're going to share with us,' reminded Gus. 'Remember, that's what you said, boss?'

Mr Big didn't answer. He puffed on his cigar thinking how poor his memory sometimes was.

9. The Great Escape

The London Underground was too complicated. Ben was frustrated that they had had to keep waiting for Ollie, and doubly frustrated that his little brother was whining. 'Are we nearly there yet?' he kept asking.

'We're halfway,' Ben shouted to his brother. They had just walked past the London Eye. Across the river Ben could see that Big Ben was saying 9.30. 'But we can't stop because the dog rescue place shuts in thirty mins.'

'I can't go any further,' whined Ollie, his little legs finally giving up. Ben stopped. He took a deep breath and rolled his eyes. He was determined to be reunited with his beloved dog and he only had thirty minutes to go. He ran back to where Ollie had sat down, arms folded and a glum look on his face.

'OK, little bro,' he said. 'You're right. It's too far and I'm going too fast. But you do understand, don't you? About Lara and everything?'

Ollie nodded. 'But my legs are only six and yours are twelve. So for me, it's twice as far.'

Ben smiled. He rummaged in his pocket and brought out a £10 note. He gave it to Sophie. 'You two go into that cafe and have a hot choc. I'll be back here with Lara in a few mins. It'll be the best New Year ever.'

Ollie managed a weak smile. 'Good idea,' he said.

Ben continued the journey, this time running, the pups by his feet.

Lara's heart was racing as she felt the baseball bat coming down so hard that it cracked her ribs. She knew the next blow would be fatal unless she managed to roll away. The bat came down on her leg and she yelped. *Grey sky. Seagulls screaming.* The sea raged below and the man came at her again.

Her back legs scrambled for a foothold. *Nothing!* She was dangling from the cliff. He came again and she let go, falling backwards, legs flailing but eyes on the face of her arch

enemy. *Mr Big. He's smiling. How can pain and suffering and death bring him so much joy?*

Lara woke with a start. She was at the dog rescue shelter. *Cage number 451 – that's it! I can remember the good bits: the family, my pups, the spy pets team and especially Benjamin. I wonder what he's doing right now? Probably thinks I'm dead. But no,* thought the dog, *I bet he's not given up. He'll be searching for me right now. And there were plenty of exciting bits,* she remembered. *The prof's amazing Spy School, some hair-raising adventures and* incredible gadgets. But right now, the scary bits are at the forefront of my mind. Lara recalled her encounter with Mr Big. Dog-napped. The clifftop. The baseball bat. She put her paw to her shoulder where he'd cut out the tracker. And my face, still swollen. Falling off the cliff. No wonder my memory blanked, she thought.

She looked at Trixie and Beyoncé. Normal dogs. They'll sit and wait until someone chooses them. It could be months. Lara remembered the sneering face of Mr Big. He told me about a crime on New Year's Eve. Big Ben. Explosions. Plural. He said the only way to stop them was to stop Big Ben at midnight. Lara looked through the office window. She knew it was New Year's Eve. The clock said 9 p.m. Three hours to save the world. I need a Spy Dog solution. First step? Escape.

Lara explained the plan one more time. 'But I don't want to fight you,' said Trixie. 'I'm a poodle; we don't really do fighting.'

'No, it's not a real fight,' said Lara. 'We're pretending. I just need to attract the attention of the lady with the keys. That's all.'

'But if we fight, they spray cold water at us,'

said Beyoncé. 'And that plays havoc with my fringe.'

Lara puffed out her cheeks in frustration. Time was ticking.

'Girls,' she said, 'for me? Just do it for me? Please?'

'But we hardly know you,' woofed Beyoncé. 'And if my hair got wet, it'd be really terrible.'

'It makes mine go frizzy,' said Trixie. 'And I really don't need extra frizz.'

I despair, thought Lara. *My own species? Sometimes they can be such a waste of space.*

'Girls,' woofed Lara, 'I've tried to be nice. But I haven't got any more time.' The retired Spy Dog raised the hair on her neck and curled her lip in a terrifying snarl. 'I'm not going to hurt you, but I need a distraction.' A throaty growl came next and she lowered her body, ready to leap at her cellmates.

Trixi yelped and made for the corner. Lara charged, head down like a bull, and Trixie somersaulted in the air. The terrified poodle started yapping. Beyoncé was next.

'Bark, extra loudly,' snarled Lara, 'or I'll mess with your hair.'

Beyonce howled like a wolf. The rest of the dogs started to get excited and within thirty seconds Battersea Dogs Home had gone barking mad.

'Keep going,' snarled Lara to her cellmates.

The lady with the keys burst out of the office. 'What on earth?' she began, hurrying along the cages trying to calm the animals. She came to Lara's cage where the dogs seemed to be fighting.

'You three,' she yelled. 'I knew this new dog would be trouble. Probably been fighting before it even got in here.' Lara continued to snarl as the lady bent down and turned on the tap. She walked towards the cage and pointed the hose at the dogs. Trixi howled like a vampire at sunrise as the water hit her hair. Lara came to the front of the cage and caught the cold water full in the face. She stood tall on her hind legs, overdoing the snarling and exposing her barrel chest.

Come closer, lady, she dared.

The lady adjusted the nozzle so that the water came out faster. She came to the bars of the cage, angry that one dog could start a riot.

'Take that you pesky mutt,' she said as Lara

finally retreated to the back of the cage, soaked
but satisfied.

The lady turned off the hose and wagged a
finger at the three dogs. 'That'll teach you,' she
said. 'No more fighting or I'll be back.'

Trixie and Beyoncé sobbed in the corner.
Lara smiled to herself. *Chaos works every time*,
she thought as she put her paw through the
bars and pulled the lady's keys towards her.

It was five minutes to ten when Ben burst
through the door. 'I'm sorry,' said the lady
behind the counter, drying herself off with a
towel, 'but we've just this minute closed.'

'But it's only five to,' he panted.

'Yes, well, we've had a little *incident*,' said the lady through a watery smile. 'The dogs got a bit overexcited. So I've bedded them down for the night.'

'But I know who I want,' said Ben, pulling the mobile from his pocket. 'This one,' he said holding up the webpage. 'This is Lara. She's my dog. Please?' he said, tears welling in his eyes. 'These puppies,' he said, 'She's their mum.'

The lady looked at the picture, one eyebrow raised. 'Lara, eh?' she said. 'She's the one we've been having trouble with.' She could see that the boy was upset. 'You will be having some trouble with her because she's not a normal dog, you see,' explained the boy. 'She's actually a spy. But more than that, she's my best friend,' he said, his voice wavering. 'We thought she was dead or dog-napped, and then we saw that she was here. We've run all the way,' he said, this time his voice breaking.

The lady felt tears welling in her own eyes. The spy bit was ridiculous, but the best friend part totally believable. She had two dogs of her own. *Family*, she thought. *Imagine if I lost them?*

She looked at the clock. 'OK then,' she sighed, turning the *Open* sign on the door to read *Closed*. 'But you're the last customer this year. And you'll have to be quick.'

Ben smiled through his tears and followed the lady out into the yard. 'Cage number 451,' she said, marching along the line. She turned to face the cage and Ben joined her, both mouths flying wide open with disbelief as they took in the scene.

'Oh my gosh, did you say 451?' asked Ben. 'This one?'

The keys were in the lock and the door was ajar. Trixie and Beyoncé were cowering at the back of the cage, whining.

'I bet my hair's gone frizzy,' whimpered Trixie. 'And my fringe must look awful,' whined Beyoncé.

'Oh my gosh indeed,' said the lady looking at Ben. 'Your dog has escaped.' She wandered into the cage and picked something up. She turned back to Ben as though she were sleep-walking. Her eyes were staring into the middle distance as she held out the piece of paper.

'Are you Ben?' she asked. 'If so, your dog's left you a note.'

10. Down to Business

Gus pulled the van up outside the Houses of Parliament. 'Double yellas, boss,' he said. 'Does that matter?'

'Triple yellas for all I care,' he said, tossing a fake disabled permit on to the dashboard. 'In view of my bad leg,' he growled as the men emerged from the van and assembled their tools. 'Bold as brass,' he reminded them as they strode up the path towards the front door. Mr Big handed his fake ID badge to the guard. It was scanned and he was let in, no questions asked. It was as expected, airport-style security, so his briefcase was placed on a conveyor and scanned.

Gus was next, his beard tickling and sweat running down his back. He plonked his toolbox on the conveyor and the guard pulled him to one side. 'Tools?' he asked.

'Err, yes,' he said, 'm'lord.'

The security man eyed Gus suspiciously. 'For what purpose?'

Gus pointed to the logo on his overalls. 'Clock repairs,' he said, trying to be bold as brass. 'Keep Big Ben bonging.'

'Three of you?' asked the guard.

'Yes three of us,' spat Mr Big. 'The big chap carries the tools, the little hairy chap does the fixing . . .'

'And yourself, sir?' asked the guard, raising an eyebrow. 'What exactly will you be doing up in the clock tower?'

Throwing you off it if you're not careful, thought Mr Big, trying to look calm. 'I'm their manager,' he smiled. 'I'm making sure they do the job properly.'

The guard seemed satisfied. He nodded and let them through. 'Clock tower is that door at the end,' he pointed, 'and there's a lot of steps!'

The professor screeched his car to a halt outside the Houses of Parliament. It was double yellows but he didn't care. His app was bleeping very loudly – *my bionic flea is in that building*.

He slammed the car door and hurried past a clock-repair van.

The old man approached the security guard and flashed his official government pass. The guard took a close look. 'I'm a friend of the prime minister, for goodness' sake,' tutted the scientist.

'And what's your business?' asked the guard.

'My business is none of yours,' reminded the scientist. 'But if you must know, I'm looking for Bob.'

'Bob?' asked the guard, looking at his list of names. 'Bob who, exactly?'

'I haven't got time to explain, my good fellow,' said the professor, trying to calm himself. 'I'm actually after a dog. And this blue dot here,' he said, holding the app for the guard to see, 'tells me the dog is in the clock tower. Top floor.'

The guard chuckled. 'No dogs allowed up there, sir,' he said. 'But there are three clock guys, making sure that New Year's Eve goes with a bang.'

'Excellent,' dismissed the professor, waddling along the corridor before striding up the stone staircase. 'I'll pop up and ask them.'

Mr Big stepped on to the balcony. 'Nice view,' he bellowed above the noise of the wind and traffic. The Houses of Parliament lay to his right and he could see Nelson standing atop his column in Trafalgar Square. Close up, the clock face was massive and he could see the minute hand moving in tiny jagged motions. He stepped back inside the tower, where the steady tick-tocking started to make him feel hypnotized. There were four clock faces looking over London and sitting in the middle was the huge bell, Big Ben. The men looked at each other and nodded. It was so beautiful that they knew words would just spoil the moment.

A huge lever with a ball on the end was in place. They knew that every fifteen minutes the cogs would whirr and the ball would strike Big Ben, signalling the passing of time. Archie opened his backpack and pulled out three pairs of earmuffs. He pointed to one of the clock faces.

'One minute to eleven,' he said. 'Get ready to be bonged.'

The men positioned their ear protectors and waited as the minute hand juddered upwards. And then it began. The ball smacked against the bell and even with ear protectors it was loud. The air vibrated, sending Archie off his feet. He half stood and then fell again on the second bong. Five bongs in and he was standing and smiling, holding on to Gus's thick arm as the air whooshed and the stone tower vibrated.

After eleven hits the lever stopped and the bell quietened, its job done. Everyone in the city had been alerted to the fact that there was one hour left of the year.

'Amaaaazing,' sang Archie, collecting the earmuffs back in. 'But we need to work quickly because it'll be ringing again in fifteen minutes. Follow me.'

The men skipped down the winding stone stairway to a room just below the bell tower. Gus produced a key and they entered the room.

'This is where it all happens,' explained Archie. 'The business end of the clock,' he said, sweeping his hand across the mass of mechanical cogs and pulleys.

The boss lit a cigar and watched. This was Archie's territory – he was a counterfeiter by trade, so good with machinery and detail. Gus laid out the tools and the small man set to work, glancing at the instructions he'd printed off. If Archie was the surgeon, Gus was his assistant.

'Spanner,' said Archie, holding out his hand. 'And screwdriver.'

There was some cursing as he struggled to loosen one of the bolts. Gus was called into

action, reaching his enormous muscled arm into the mechanism, before Archie took over once more.

'Small spanner,' he requested. He reached right into the cogs and twisted. 'And finally, the iPad.'

There was a knock at the door. 'Hello,' came a voice. 'Is that GM451?' The door swung open and Professor Cortex stared at the men. There was a moment of blinking as the criminals gawped back. The scientist didn't have time to yell because Gus had him in a headlock.

'Steady on, old chap,' panted the scientist. 'You're making my ears burn. I'm struggling to breathe. And where's GM451?' came his muffled cry. 'And Bob?'

Archie got to work with the tape and in less than sixty seconds the professor was gagged and trussed up. His face and eyes gave off waves of silent anger. Gus had just dragged the old man out of sight when the door swung open again and the security guard from downstairs entered the room.

'Just checking you're OK,' said the man. 'Oh, and this is a no-smoking clock tower,' he reminded Mr Big.

The master criminal raised an eyebrow. 'Absolutely,' he said, grinding his cigar into the stone wall. 'I'm sorry,' he lied. He loved lying. It was in his top five favourite things, just behind cruelty, murder, torture and blackmail. 'Won't happen again,' he said in a double fib. 'And, anyway, I'm giving up,' he said, going for a hat-trick of total deceit.

The security guard looked a little suspiciously at the iPad. The clock was regularly checked and repaired, but it was an old mechanism and the other guys used proper tools.

Gus's fists clenched, waiting for the instruction from Mr Big.

'It's like, you know, we want to get the time spot on,' said Archie. 'So we're consulting modern technology to check the exact time.'

The man nodded. 'Don't suppose you've seen an old chap in a white coat?' he asked. 'He was heading this way, looking for a dog, apparently,' he chuckled.

'A man looking for a dog, you say,' repeated Mr Big as Gus aimed a kick to quieten the muffled professor. 'I can assure you, sir, there aren't any dogs up here.'

The man disappeared and Archie breathed a sigh of relief. 'Now, iPad, please?' he reminded. 'We're running out of time.'

'Carefully does it,' said Archie to himself as he secured the iPad in place, connecting the blue and red wires. He switched it on, tapped at the screen and looked up at Mr Big. 'Exactly at midnight?' he asked.

'New Year's Day. At the first bong of Big Ben,' replied the criminal mastermind with a nod. 'For maximum publicity.'

Archie tapped at the iPad. Gus and Mr Big

watched as he slid the modern device underneath the ancient cogs. 'Out of sight, just in case,' he said. 'The job is, as they say, a guddun.'

Gus packed the tools away.

'The iPad's part of a wireless device,' explained Archie as he applied an extra layer of tape to the professor's mouth. 'An invention you'd be proud of, as a matter of fact. The boss here, he don't just want to make money on this crime – he wants to be famous. So, when the clock strikes midnight, the sound waves will activate Wi-Fi controlled detonators hidden in barrels of gunpowder in every single prison in the country.' The professor's muffled protests and furrowed forehead were telling Archie off. 'And you, old man, you're lucky.'

'Ummm umm?' gagged the scientist.

'Yes, lucky,' said Archie. 'Because you, sir, are getting the best seat in the house.' The three criminals skipped down the steps to the bottom of the tower. The security guard opened the door to let them out.

'All sorted?' he asked.

'Everything's going according to plan,' smiled Mr Big, disappointed that for once he was having to tell the truth. 'My boys have made sure that there will be something wonderful to see at midnight on New Year's Eve. We're hoping that lots of parties will go with a bang.'

'That's what we want,' beamed the security guard. 'Big Ben always sees in the New Year with a boom!'

Mr Big thought ahead. His mind raced to the first bong of New Year's Eve and swirled with the thought of how happy he was going to be.

'And because you've been such a gent, helping us out and all that, we've got a special something for you.'

'Special? For me?' The man blushed.

Gus had popped out to the van and was rolling a barrel across the courtyard. He picked it up and raised it to his shoulder, plonking it inside the doorway.

'Home Office Ale,' read the man. 'For me?'

'For you, mate,' nodded Mr Big. 'And the wider team who are all having to work on New Year's evening. On one condition.'

He looked deep into the man's eyes. 'No drinkies until after that first bong of midnight. Deal?'

The security guard felt uneasy. Mr Big's good eye was staring straight at him and his glass one was slightly wonky, looking over the man's shoulder. There was something about those eyes that meant you didn't want to disagree.

'Deal,' grinned the man.

'Happy New Year,' growled Mr Big as he and his henchmen strode back to the van.

11. The Truth Hurts

It was 11 p.m. on New Year's Eve. The children, Spud, Star and Shakespeare assembled in the professor's London lab. Everything was deathly quiet. Ben switched on the lights and they flickered into life.

'Lara left me this note,' he said. 'She knew I'd not give up.'

His sister read the swirly writing. 'Beware. Big's in town. Big Ben bong, goes bang at 12 2-nite. Mission: Stop the clock before it bongs. Go to prof's lab and find some inventions/gadgets to help,' she read. Her face scrunched up in confusion. 'What on earth does that all mean?'

The pups were wagging. 'Mum's alive, for one thing,' whined Star. 'But if Mr Big's in London we'd better watch out.'

'Look, I don't really know, sis,' said Ben. 'But Lara wants us to stop Big Ben striking midnight. I bet this whole dog-napping thing is some sort of sinister Mr Big plot. He probably wanted her out of the way.'

'Let's just call the police,' suggested Ollie.

Ben looked a little surprised at the simplicity of the idea. He nodded, tapping 999 into his keypad.

'Hello, police?' he began. 'I want to report a probable explosion when Big Ben strikes midnight. That's like in less than an hour,' he said glancing at the time on his mobile. Everyone hushed as the lady spoke to him. 'Where did I get my information? Well, I found a note. In fact I've got it here,' he said, waving it in his other hand.

'Who's it from?' he repeated. Ben put his hand over the phone. 'She wants to know who wrote the note,' he whispered.

'Tell her the truth,' Sophie mouthed back. 'And nothing but the truth,' she added, thinking it sounded about right.

'It's a note from . . . my dog,' blurted Ben. 'But, wait a minute, because I know that sounds silly. She's a Spy Dog, you see, so she can read and write and stuff.'

'And she can cook pancakes,' shouted Ollie.

'Sorry, that was my little brother,' said Ben. 'But actually she can. Blueberry ones.' he added, wishing he hadn't. He paused while the lady spoke to him.

'Wasting police time?' shouted Ben down the phone. 'Of course I'm not. And, no, I haven't been drinking . . . I'm twelve!' He looked at his siblings and pets. 'She's cut me off,' he said. 'So much for the truth.'

Just then the lift started whirring. 'Somebody's coming,' whispered Sophie. 'Into this deserted laboratory at nearly midnight. What if it's Mr Big?'

Ollie squealed. 'Quick, everyone, hide,' he said, climbing into a cupboard.

Ben ran for the lightswitch, plunging the lab back into darkness and the children and animals fell to their knees behind benches and tables. Silence prevailed as the lift ascended to the fifth floor with a *ping*. Ben felt his heart beating as he gripped a glass beaker, ready to throw it at Mr Big.

The lift doors parted and there stood his dog.

She smelled her family before she saw them: three children, two puppies and a cat, hurling themselves at her.

Lara's wag was well and truly back.

It took a while for Sophie to stifle her tears. She kept looking at Lara, saw the pups snuggled under their mum's tummy, and the tears started again. Ollie was whooping and Ben had a massive grin, but he knew there was a mission and that time was ticking.

'OK, team,' he announced, 'it's great to have Lara back, but we've got a world to save. We have to stop Big Ben chiming midnight.'

Lara nodded, looking round the laboratory. It was a typical professor mess.

'What are we looking for, exactly?' asked Ollie.

'Anything that will help get us into the clock tower,' said Ben. He opened a cupboard and pulled out a few folders. *Inventions* said one, *Cunning plans* another. Ben wracked his brains, thinking back through the adventures.

'All the professor's inventions are in this room. What have we used that would be useful this time round?' he said aloud.

'There's no way they're going to let us in at ground level,' said Sophie, 'so the only way would be if we climb the tower on the outside.' She looked round and nobody seemed keen on that idea. 'Or we come at it from above.'

Ben was lost in thought for a second. 'Sis,' he said, 'let's allocate tasks and do both.'

He pulled some suckers from a drawer. 'Puss, you're a natural climber. Stick these on your paws and these little suckers might get you to the top.'

Shakespeare looked a little unsure; Sophie even more so. 'Quickly,' said the boy, 'it's 11.30.'

'And then there's this,' he said, pulling the sheet off the professor's drone. 'It says in this folder that it's a window-cleaning drone, especially developed for cleaning skyscrapers.'

Ollie rolled his eyes. 'We don't want to clean Big Ben,' he said.

'No, but we need to get someone to the top of it,' urged his brother. 'It's remote controlled. If I remove this bucket,' he said, rearranging the device, 'we have room for a passenger.'

'And they can wear one of these,' smiled Sophie, holding a piece of red fabric in the air. 'Remember, Shakespeare wore one of these flying suits when he rescued me once. My little hero,' she said, rubbing the cat's nose. 'We raise a passenger high into the air and they swoop using the flying suit.'

The pups both raised their paws in excitement. 'I'll do it,' they woofed together.

Lara looked at them and shook her head.

'Too dangerous, guys,' she woofed. 'This is not a Spy Pups job. I may be retired from active service, but I think this is one last mission for a fully qualified Spy Dog.'

12. The Swoop

Spud had set up the professor's lab as mission headquarters. Shakespeare had already been dispatched, with four suckers and a headcam.

'North wall of the clock tower,' said Lara. 'We don't know if it's possible, but we'll never know unless we try. This is not a drill, Agent Cat, this is the real thing.' Lara had given the puss a chance to back out, but Shakespeare had refused, running off into the London streets to get started, and a large TV screen beamed pictures into the lab from his catcam.

Lara struggled into her flying suit, her broken ribs making her wince in pain. If the situation had been any less serious they might have stopped to chuckle as they zipped her up. 'Ouch, my hair,' she winced as Sophie apologized.

'And these goggles,' said Sophie, fitting them over her swollen face, 'have a camera fitted so you'll be on TV screen number two. Remember, when you let go of the drone, spread your legs and the loose fabric will allow you to glide.'

'It's not flying,' reminded Star. 'A bit like hang-gliding. Spread your legs wide and you'll slow down, bring them in and you'll freefall.'

'I know the theory,' barked Lara. 'Shame I've never had time to practise!'

'So puss is climbing from the bottom and you're coming at the clock face from above. Not sure if you'll be able to steer correctly or what you'll do when you get there. But, hey, if anyone can do it, you can, girl.'

Ben gave Lara a huge hug. 'It's so good to have you back,' he said. 'Your country needs you. Go, girl.'

Ben opened the door and stepped out on to the balcony, the orange glow of the city shimmering all around. Rain was hammering down and lightning streaked the sky.

'Big Ben is about half a mile that way, I think,' shouted the boy, jabbing a finger to the left. 'I'll get this thing as high as I can and you'll have to glide in from there, OK?'

Lara pulled her goggles into place and nodded. She squeezed into the small space where the bucket had been and fixed her paws round a bar to hold on as best she could. Ben pressed the ignition button. Eight sets of tiny helicopter blades whirred into action. 'Now then,' he said, looking at the remote. 'I think this one will . . .'

'Whoa,' whined Lara, almost losing her grip as the drone juddered upwards and then went left and right. The dog hung in the air before scrabbling back into place.

'Err, sorry,' said Ben. 'I've got it now. Left,

right and up or down. A bit like my Play-Station.'

'Except this is no game,' woofed Lara as her best friend pushed the stick forward and the blades gradually lifted the dog higher into the air.

She tried not to look as terrified as she felt as the children waved and eventually disappeared, becoming tiny dots. Lara dangled over the lights of London, drenched to her bones.

This is ridiculously high, she thought. She craned her neck and lightning crackled across the sky. She saw the London Eye to her left. *And Big Ben's very near that*. Time was ticking and her heart pounding. *I reckon it's about eight minutes till midnight. Here goes!*

She unhooked her legs from the bar and plummeted towards earth.

The cat had used the cover of darkness to scamper through the railings and across the grass. He stood at the bottom of the Elizabeth Tower and looked up, lightning flashing across the sky and rain bouncing off the grass. *Gulp. I like climbing trees, but this is a different matter*. He fixed the suckers to his feet and stood on his hind legs.

He threw his left front paw at the wall and it stuck. His right went as high as it would go and he was dangling. His back left followed and before long he had developed quite a technique.

The cat looked upwards, the tower rising into the rain. *Fifteen minutes to go.*

At HQ, all eyes were on screen number two. Lara was falling fast.

'Stop flapping; you're not a bird! Extend your arms, or legs – whatever,' shouted Sophie at the screen. Almost on cue the dog did just that and the camera showed the falling motion suddenly stop and the dog swoop – *not very elegant*, thought Lara, *but, hey, I can glide!*

She lifted her right paw a little and her body turned left, sweeping through the rain towards the orange lights of the Houses of Parliament.

Shakespeare was exhausted. His legs screamed in pain. *And I'm only half way! I'm not sure if I can get all the way*, he thought. He took a thirty-second breather, a bedraggled feline hanging above London. He thought about Mr Big's evil plan. *We're not sure what it is*, he thought. *But it's bound to be horrible. Onwards and upwards*, he thought, hoping Lara was having more success coming from above.

★

Lara had got the hang of it. She saw thousands of people gathering on the river bank, waiting for the midnight fireworks. *London is buzzing!* She glided past the London Eye, noticing that the big wheel was full of party revellers, keen to be at the top as Big Ben ushered in the New Year. Every car was full, with people peering across the river at the big clock.

Sammy and his sister had come to London with their grandma for a once in a lifetime opportunity of being on the world's biggest big wheel at the stroke of midnight. There were four minutes to go as the dog floated by. Lara caught the little boy's eye and saluted.

'Evening,' she woofed as she sped by. Sammy tugged his grandma's jumper. 'Gran,' he said, 'you know dogs in London. Do they wear superhero outfits?'

His grandma took her eyes from her binoculars and looked down at her grandson. 'Of course not,' she said. 'London dogs are like our dogs. Just ordinary.'

'Oh,' he said, looking confused. 'But they're good flyers, though.'

Gran chuckled. 'Here; have a look at the view through these,' she said, handing the little

boy her binoculars. 'It's been a very long day for you and you're up very late.'

Sammy pressed against the glass and peered through the binoculars. 'Cooool.' He watched the dog swoop across the river towards Big Ben.

The cat had defied gravity and got there first. He clambered on to the ledge of the east face of the clock, his chest heaving with the effort. *Soaked through! Now what?*

The children watched screen number one, as the cat glanced all round. Left and right were beautiful views of night-time London and down was a very long drop. The huge clock face was illuminated as Shakespeare looked up. 'Two minutes to go,' shouted Ben at the screen. 'Do something. You have to stop it bonging.'

He jumped off the ledge into the clock tower. 'There is no time to admire the view,' yelled Ben at the screen. The cat leaped onto a window sill and then into the room where the professor was lying, trussed up like a turkey.

'Oh my gosh,' said Sophie, her hand to her mouth. 'There's the prof!'

The cat ran to the old man and scratched the tape from his mouth.

'Don't worry about me, Agent Cat,' the professor shouted. 'You have to stop the clock. If it strikes midnight there will be terrible explosions. Lots of them. I haven't got time to explain.' His eyes were wild with terror. 'Stop that clock!'

The cat had been trained by the best. He'd attended the finest Spy School in the world and he was fully prepared – for nearly everything! He ran through possible courses of action and only one seemed to be right. He clambered back out on to the ledge into the howling gale, the city sprawling below. The cat suckered his feet on to the clock face and began climbing again. *Both hands are pointing upwards. So 12 o'clock is where I have to be.*

The interview with the headteacher whose New Year's resolution was to make school 'like Christmas every day, with turkey dinner and everything' had finished and the BBC newsreader put on her excited look. She turned to camera one. 'And with ninety seconds to go before the end of the year, it's time to cross over to the grandfather of time. We're going live to Big Ben where I'm told,' she said, forgetting her excited face and putting on her puzzled one, 'that we have some breaking news. Is that right, Justin? What can you tell us from central London?'

The camera flicked to a huge close-up of the face of Big Ben, where Shakespeare had made it to the hands of the clock and attached himself to the big hand. He was heaving as hard as he could, trying to pull the hand backwards.

'With less than a minute to go,' said the reporter, 'we seem to have what can only be described as an incident,' he said. 'It seems there's what looks like a cat up there. It appears to have boots on its tiny paws and what might be best described as a hat with a torch on its head. And if the pictures are to be believed, it's hanging on to the minute hand.'

'Has the cat stopped the clock?' asked the newsreader.

'Unconfirmed reports suggest not,' said the reporter. 'It looks as though the cat is wrestling with the long hand, but that the puss doesn't weigh enough to actually stop it. But remember, these are, as yet, unconfirmed pictures of an unconfirmed cat. But what a cat is doing up there, and why it is trying to stop the clock, is anyone's unconfirmed guess.'

'Or indeed, how it got up there,' chuckled the lady. 'I think we once had three blind mice climbing a clock,' she said, filling time before the fireworks. 'And now in true panto style, we have a puss in boots.'

13. Countdown

Mr Big and his henchmen sat in the underground lair, glued to the TV as they waited for the big bang of midnight. He raised his glass. 'The finest bubbly for the finest criminal team. I propose a toast.'

Archie and Gus raised their glasses, ready to join in.

'To me,' sang Mr Big. 'Soon to be the world's most famous criminal of all time.'

'To you,' chorused Archie and Gus.

'In one minute, Big Ben will strike midnight and the noise will trigger 136 barrels to go bang. That's a dirty great hole in every prison in England and Wales, allowing 180,000 dirty great criminals to walk away into the night.'

'It sure is a beautiful plan,' agreed Archie. 'And our army of private security guards are recruited and ready to start work at 9 a.m. tomorrow morning. I love it that you have created the problem . . .'

'And the solution,' purred Mr Big sipping his fizz. 'And the final keg is at the Houses of Parliament. So when Big Ben strikes it will blow itself up.'

'Live on the telly,' smiled Gus. 'I like that, boss. It's a nice touch. Like not just a teeny bit naughty, but proper genuine evil.'

Mr Big lengthened his neck in pride. He loved compliments. He also usually liked breaking news, as it was often some sort of fabulous disaster or murder. But when the newsreader announced that there was an incident at Big Ben, he was not best pleased. The TV cut to a picture of a cat hanging on to the minute hand and he snorted so hard on his champagne that it fizzed down his nose. 'What the –' he began. 'Is that even possible?'

The children were sitting in mission HQ in silence. Shakespeare had made it, but his weight wasn't enough to stop the clock. His body was swinging as he tried to turn back time. 'I'm wet, I'm exhausted and I'm failing,' he yowled at the

top of his voice. He tried to put his foot between the big and little hands to stop the forward motion, but the hand kept inching upwards.

The studio audience were enthralled. Millions of people around the world held their breath as the countdown to midnight began. People at parties stopped partying and counted. Those on the banks of the river had ten seconds to wait until their fireworks were lit. 'Ten, nine, eight . . .' they chanted.

Lara had the clock tower in her sights but wasn't sure how accurate she'd be. Ben and the children watched screen two. 'She's coming at it incredibly fast,' said Ben. 'In fact, I'd say far too fast . . .'

'Seven, six . . .' chanted the onlookers.

'There are indeed very strange goings-on as the seconds tick away,' commented the reporter, 'the cat seems to be trying to stop the clock . . . but, whoa, wait a second, the incident has just got a whole lot stranger . . .'

Lara hit the tower with a massive force that knocked the wind out of her. Lightning struck as she scrambled for a foothold. She'd missed the clock face by a whisper, landing on the ledge above the clock. Her outfit was caught on a nail and she was momentarily lost in no-man's-land, her front paws reaching for the ledge and her back legs kicking wildly against the clock face. The fabric ripped and she dangled lower.

'Four, three . . .' chanted a million party-goers across the land.

'The cat has been joined by a dog . . .' jabbered the reporter.

Lara heard a cat meowing below and she

wriggled to loosen herself. *It's a very long way down*, she thought, *but I've got no choice. The mog isn't heavy enough. He needs me.* The dog wriggled, there was a massive ripping sound as her outfit tore and she dropped three metres and caught hold of the cat.

'Two, one . . .'

Archie nervously pulled his knees under his chin and grabbed a cushion to hide behind. Gus stood, face like thunder, punching one hand into the other. Ten seconds ago the criminals had been relaxed. Then the cat had appeared and they'd winced.

'Cat's not heavy enough,' smirked the mastermind, refilling his champagne glass. 'We'll be OK cos that dog fell off the cliff . . .'

His sentence was cut short as Lara plunged from the sky, superhero style, and added her weight to the clock hand.

'Is that the dead dog you were talking about?' asked Gus.

Mr Big's champagne glass shattered in his hand. The TV zoomed in for a close-up. Lara's face was still swollen, but there was no mistaking her sticky-up ear. Mr Big had been proud of firing the bullet that holed her ear, but right now he was wishing the bullet had been a little more fatal.

Fifty million party poppers exploded across England. Champagne corks popped and music started as the citizens saw in the New Year. The city sky lit up with fireworks. Nobody noticed that Big Ben was silent. The dog and cat scrabbled to hold on. The big hand started to groan under the weight and then, as Lara pulled hard, it ticked backwards.

'It's moving,' woofed Lara. 'We've done it!' The dog wrestled harder and the clock went backwards faster.

The children watched the news footage as the time went backwards to 11.45 and then downhill very fast to 11.30. Ben gulped. The TV footage showed a dog and cat now dangling from the minute hand.

Mission HQ was still beaming from the pet-cams, showing a magnificent view and a very long drop.

'Hold on, girl,' yelled Ben.

Sophie was hiding behind her fingers. 'She can't hold on – she's only got paws,' she wailed.

The newsreader was getting very excited and then the dog disappeared off camera and the TV screen quickly returned to a sky full of fireworks.

Lara's flying suit was ripped. She spread her wings and the fabric flapped by. Sophie squealed and Ben's mouth gaped as they watched Lara's pet-cam.

It was a long way down and Lara was amazed

at how many memories flashed before her eyes in those final moments. *Twenty missions. Some fabulous adventures and the world's first ever qualified Spy Dog. Sniffing out baddies and solving crimes,* she thought as she plummeted. *Nice to end on a big one.* Her ears flapped and the ground loomed. *Mostly happy memories. And so nice to have found a family that I love. And a boy*, she thought, *who really is a dog's best friend.*

TV screens one and two went blank and Ben sobbed. He didn't care that his dog had saved the world.

14. The Final Chapter

'The End!', typed Tyrone, putting the pencil down and giving his mouth a well-earned rest.

Phew! A spine-tingling story that ends on a cliff-hanger, he thought to himself. *I hope my teacher likes it.* He noticed that his brothers and sisters had finished working and were upstairs watching a movie.

Ty spellchecked his work before clicking 'save' and then 'print'. He heard the upstairs printer whirr into action. For once he was really looking forward to school. *I can't wait to read my story out*, he wagged. *And, the best thing of all, it's true! My grandma really did save the world. Well, the country, at least.*

Sophie and Ollie wandered into the kitchen. Ty noticed that his mum and Uncle Spud were already at the door, wagging excitedly.

'He's just texted,' said Sophie. 'Ben. He's off the bus and walking down the road. He says, *Get that kettle on. Home in 2*, she read. The teenager flicked the kettle on just as the door burst open and her big brother slumped into the kitchen, dumping a huge rucksack on the floor. Star and Spud went wagging mad, with Spud unable to resist a quick jump up at the young man.

'Pleased to see you too, buddy,' he said, 'but please let me through the door before you lick me to death.'

The pups heard the commotion and bundled down the stairs. Sophie had a quick hug with her beloved big brother before the kitchen became a seething mass of wagging tails and lolling tongues. Ollie started telling his big brother about a new computer game, Sophie was asking him about university and the dogs were giddy with glee.

Ty had sprinted upstairs to fetch his homework, grabbing it in his teeth and scampering back downstairs, tail wagging. He waited until Ben had got his cup of tea and made it to one of the stools in the kitchen.

'Uni's great,' he beamed. 'Sof, you're gonna love it when it's your turn, but,' he said, looking round the kitchen at the array of pets and people, 'there's nowhere quite like home.'

He winced as he took a sip of too-hot tea. 'What's this, little fella?' he said, as Ty dragged a sheaf of papers across the kitchen table.

Homework, wagged the smallest puppy. *Hot off the press. Excuse the slobber*, he wagged, *but it's my best homework evs. And I think you'll like the subject matter.*

Ben turned the papers the right way round and slurped at the hot tea again. 'Homework?' he said. 'Ty, I'm impressed.'

The puppy wagged so hard his body swayed from side to side. 'Might be a few typos, but it's all my own work.'

'Based on a true story,' began Ben, reading aloud. 'It started in Hurtmore Mega-Max Ultimate Security Prison. The guard slid the bolt and opened the hatch . . .' He looked at the pup. 'Did you write this, little guy?'

'He's been sitting here for hours,' said Ollie. 'Never known Ty to be quite so keen on anything.'

Except custard creams, thought Spud, eyeing the biscuit tin and thinking how rude it was for Ben not to be offered one with his cuppa.

The teenager scanned the first page. 'Wow,' he said, 'this is really good, Ty. It's got the underwater mobile phone,' he said. 'And Big Ben,' he said flicking through a few more pages. 'Is it the story of Lara's final mission? The one where Mr Big threw her off a cliff and she lost her memory?'

Ty's tail went from side to side and his head up and down.

'I used mum's credit card to book train tickets and I took us all to London. Mum sure was angry when she got home,' remembered Ben. 'But then she was angry every time we went on a mission.'

'It was an amazing adventure,' said Ollie. 'I was only small but I remember watching the

TV at midnight. And Lara hanging on to the face of Big Ben. And . . .' All of a sudden the room felt drained.

'I'll read it all the way through later,' said Ben. 'It's such a shame about the sad ending.'

'At least Mr Big got caught,' said Ollie. 'Bob the flea stuck to his task and as soon as Big came up for air, he was nabbed.'

'And this time he's stayed nabbed,' sighed Sophie. 'Mega-max-ultra-hyper-plus I think they call his new prison cell.'

The children winced as they remembered the live TV footage of their beloved dog falling from the hands of Big Ben. Sophie had Shakespeare in her arms, holding him tightly. 'Pusskins here got away with a few scratches and bruises,' she said.

And a broken jaw, thought the cat, resisting the urge to yawn.

Ben sniffed. He turned to Ty's last page once again, reading aloud: 'Her ears flapped and the ground loomed. Happy memories. And so nice to have found a family that I love.' The boy's voice broke a little and he sniffed a little louder before reading the last sentence, '*And a boy*, she thought, *who really is a dog's best friend*.'

Ben blinked hard. The room was silent. 'Where is she?' he asked his sister.

Sophie nodded towards the lounge. 'Having a snooze, I expect,' she smiled.

The dogs and children left Ben to it. Sophie turned back to page one and started reading Ty's story to the assembled crowd.

Ben stood in the hallway and composed himself. He turned the doorknob and pushed the lounge door open. His head peeped into the room. Professor Cortex was snoring gently, mouth open, newspaper on his lap. Lara was wide awake, her tail thumping the chair and a silly doggy grin across her face. The old dog removed her spectacles and spread her arms wide.

Ben felt tears in his eyes as man and his best friend had a silent hug.

Have you read the Spy Cat adventures? Don't miss Shakespeare's less than purrrrfect encounter with Lara and the pups! Turn over for a sneak peek of *Summer Shocker*! . . .

2. Second-in-Command

Shakespeare woke with a start, his green eyes instantly wide and his claws extended. He scanned the room and his heart gradually stopped pounding. When you'd spent weeks living rough like Shakespeare had, you learnt to always be alert and ready to run – or fight. *After the last few weeks I've had*, thought the cat, *I'm lucky to be alive at all!* He looked around at Sophie's bedroom – pink curtains, cream walls and a pair of fluffy slippers. *Perfect*. Shakespeare stretched out luxuriously, hooking his claws into the super-soft bedding. *Peace and quiet and a nice comfy duvet, at last. What more could a feline want?*

The window was open and Shakespeare could hear some barking outside. His whiskers twitched nervously. *Bad memories*. He leapt effortlessly up on to the sill, being careful to stay hidden behind the curtain, and spied on the meeting below. *What a strange gathering of animals*. He looked at the black and white dog standing at the front of the group, clearly in charge. *She's the one who lives in this house*, Shakespeare realized. He always scampered away before she came back into the house, but he'd seen the children playing with her and petting her. He'd tried not to pay too much attention to the obvious love between them all. Shakespeare had no time for that sort of thing.

Her name was Lara. *Strange markings*, he thought. *And an even stranger ear arrangement*, he noticed as Lara's bullet-holed ear stood proudly to attention. Shakespeare listened intently. So she was a Spy Dog – whatever that meant. He wasn't even sure what a 'neighbourhood-watch team' actually was, but what appeared to be a competition to choose a leader to look after things while Lara was on holiday would be interesting to watch either way. It was always good to know who the competition was on your patch. He scanned the group below; there didn't seem to be anyone worth Shakespeare's attention. *But then,* thought the cat, *a life of action and adventure isn't really my thing*. Shakespeare was a loner. He only looked out for number one now. He cast an eye back to the warm bed that seemed to be calling him. *That's my thing!*

He listened to Lara's instructions, stretching a back leg and licking between his claws while he did so. 'The test is very simple. It's a feline versus canine challenge. We need to see who's cleverest, bravest and most energetic.'

Shakespeare continued listening and licking, his sandpapery tongue cleaning between his toes. 'Imagine there's a fire on the first floor of number 22. And there's a child asleep in the upstairs bedroom.'

'*Yikes!*' woofed the soppy-looking chocolate Lab. 'Best get there quick,' he said, bounding off towards the garden gate.

'Archie,' Lara bellowed. 'Heel, boy. I said *imagine*. Come back here and listen carefully to the instructions.'

Shakespeare sniggered. *Dogs are so stupid*.

'Yes, boss,' he woofed apologetically. 'But what about the fire?'

Lara sighed and shook her head. Shakespeare was surprised to see her eye the tortoiseshell cat with what looked like hope. *Interesting, not automatically rooting for her own species*.

'There's an *imaginary* baby at number 22,' Lara continued. 'And an *imaginary* fire. The first one to get into the house, upstairs, rescue the child and bring it back here is the winner, right?'

Archie looked chastened. 'Yes, boss.'

'I'm ready,' miaowed Connie, giving Archie a competitive sideways glance.

'Then what are you waiting for? Go!' woofed Lara as the cat and dog sprinted off in opposite directions.

Thirty seconds later Archie came panting back. 'Which is number 22?' he woofed.

Lara jabbed her paw after the cat, who was already halfway down the street. Archie bounded after her, a chocolate-brown bundle of enthusiasm.

Shakespeare watched lazily from above. He'd stopped licking but his back leg was still outstretched, in striking distance if the race got boring. The competition had become slightly less interesting now it was clear that the cat was going to wipe the floor with the daft dog.

Shakespeare had no time for dogs – *not stupid ones, not bossy ones like Lara, not vicious ones on the street and especially not the dog that got me evicted from my family*. It hurt him to think about it but sometimes he couldn't do anything else. Bad memories just popped into his head. The little girl had loved him so much. *A bit too much*, he considered. *So much that the dog got jealous. I just wanted a quiet family life but the mutt picked a huge fight, and when we were pulled apart I accidentally caught my owner with my claws and that was pretty much it.*

Shakespeare winced as he remembered being shouted at by the lady. *And the little girl was crying.* He'd then been palmed off on an elderly relative, far away from the little girl and his family. They probably meant well but meals were scarce and it just wasn't the same. Shakespeare had decided there and then that he would go it alone. He was going to survive all by himself. *So I left.*

He remembered catching sight of himself in a shop window two weeks later. *A stray!* he thought. *Imagine! Pampered puss to mangy moggy. Skinny ribs showing through my ginger fur. Homeless. Loveless. Living on the streets.*

Shakespeare shook his head, getting rid of the

memories. He'd soon learnt to toughen up. There were some angry dogs and very territorial cats in the neighbourhood to help him do just that. He looked in the bedroom mirror and admired his tummy, now puffed out with pride. His glossy fur – ginger except for three white feet – gleamed, and his green eyes and perky whiskers shone with health. *There's always an upside*, he considered, raising an eyebrow and giving a throaty yowl. *I'm a streetwise moggie*, he thought. *Grown up fast! I steal what I can, when I can. I don't need friends, or people, or a family. I'm a ginger ninja, it's me against the world.*

He was pleased with his current 'home'. *Three days and nights here*, he thought. *And nobody's rumbled me yet*. He'd decided to keep the family at arm's length. The little girl, Sophie, seemed friendly enough and had petted him in the garden, but so far so good. It was better that he didn't make attachments like before. Best to blend into the background. Hunt at night and find a nice snuggly duvet during the day.

Shakespeare looked back at the indentation in the duvet, imagining it might still be warm. *In a minute*, he promised. *The action below is just hotting up.*

DISCOVER THE OTHER BOOKS IN THE SPY PETS SERIES ...